# PROTECTING HER WITNESS

## SARAH HAMAKER

ISBN: 978-1-7332579-3-0

Cover design and interior layout by Hannah Linder Designs.

"May the God of hope fill you with all joy and peace in believing, so that by the power of the Holy Spirit you may abound in hope." Romans 15:13 (ESV)

# CHAPTER 1

U .S. Marshal Chalissa Manning settled into a steady pace as she ran the gravel loop ringing Burke Lake. She noted the mile marker as she swerved around a mom power-walking while pushing a jogging stroller. Whitney Houston belted "I Wanna Dance With Somebody" into her earbuds, the pulsating beat from the 1980s hit in rhythm with her stride. Saturday morning sunlight streamed through the trees lining the pathway. Another mile marker flashed by. Good, she was on pace to finish a 5K run in nineteen minutes.

She enjoyed running, loved being wrapped in her own world while the miles zipped by. So far, her transfer from the St. Louis, Missouri, office to Arlington, Virginia, had gone smoothly. After four years in St. Louis, she'd been ready for a different city and more challenging opportunities in her career with the U.S. Marshal's Witness Protection Service. For her, the career clock ticked a little louder, given she had become a Marshal shortly before her thirtieth birthday, while most of her colleagues had entered the service directly after college graduation. Her previous work with troubled youth in residential treatment centers had made her a good fit for witness protection, but being older than most of the other newbies meant she had more to prove—and less time to do it if she wanted to make the Marshals her career. Which she did.

"Help!" a male voice shouted as Chalissa came up on the marina parking lot. "My son's missing!"

Without hesitation, she veered off the path and into the parking lot, stopping her music and pulling her earbuds out. Several groups of people stood in small clusters near the fishing pier. A tall man wearing jeans and a long-sleeved flannel shirt topped by a vest with multiple pockets approached one of the clusters, his voice raised enough for Chalissa to hear.

"Have you seen my son?" The group shook their heads collectively, and the man moved onto another group, asking the same question and receiving the same reply.

Chalissa jogged up to him and touched his arm as the man turned away from the group. "Sir? Maybe I can help you."

The man whipped around so fast he nearly bumped into her. "My son's gone. He was here just a few minutes ago," his voice cracked. He swallowed hard, then continued, "I've got to find him."

"Okay, we'll find him. Tell me your name." Chalissa pitched her voice low and soothing to project calm in the midst of this man's personal storm.

"Titus. Titus Davis." Mr. Davis started to walk away, but Chalissa plucked at his sleeve to bring him to a halt.

"Mr. Davis, my name is Chalissa Manning." She waited until she had his attention once more. "I'm with the U.S. Marshal Service."

She pointed to indicate her cropped leggings and baggy T-shirt. "I'm obviously not here on official Marshal business, but let me help you find your son."

"You're with the Marshals?" Mr. Davis's shoulders relaxed a little at her nod. "Thank goodness."

"Have you called the police?"

"No." He shot a hand through his hair, sending the brown strands every-which-way but didn't volunteer any more information.

"How long would you estimate your son's been missing?" Chalissa took her phone out of its arm band and opened the notes app.

"Five minutes." Mr. Davis had returned his gaze to scanning the area.

"Mr. Davis." Chalissa waited until the man looked at her. He had a very attractive face, with its strong jawline and short-cropped beard. Chalissa mentally shook her head. The man had a son, which meant he either had a wife or a significant other. "I know you want to look for your son, but these questions will help us find him."

"I'm really worried." Mr. Davis swiped at his eyes. "He's only seven and on the spectrum."

"He has autism?" She blurted out her question before thinking, as memories slammed into her.

"Yes, it's not severe, but it does impact the way Sam interacts with people," Mr. Davis said. "He doesn't read social cues well, and can be too trusting."

"In what way?" A vision of Brandon engaging cashiers, dog walkers, and anyone else who came to his attention zipped across her mind.

"If someone asked Sam to help him look for a lost puppy, he'd do it in a flash." He rubbed his chin. "Even though we've discussed the dangers of going off with a stranger over and over again. Listen, I really need to go look for him."

Chalissa shook her head as if the movement could clear her mind from thoughts of Brandon, but the pain was just as sharp as it had been sixteen years ago. But Brandon wasn't here, and Sam needed her help. "Please bear with me. The more info I can gather, the quicker we can involve more people in looking for your son."

Her words succeeded in stopping him from walking away, but he balanced lightly on the balls of his feet, ready to leave in an instant. Better get on with her questions. "What was Sam wearing?"

"He had on jeans, sneakers, a long-sleeved blue T-shirt, and a bright orange fishing vest."

She jotted down the description. "Hair, eye color, height?"

"His hair is a little lighter brown than mine," Mr. Davis gestured to his head. "His eyes are brown and he wears glasses. They're bright green, the kind that wrap all the way around the back of his head. And he's about yea big." He held out his hand to indicate close to three feet.

"Thank you, that's very helpful. Where did you last see him?"

"It was down by the pier." He pointed to the fishing pier. "We had set up to fish—see the blue camping chairs about midway down on the left side?"

"I see them." She noted the location, then added the information to her notes.

"Sam realized he'd dropped his favorite lure. He'd been holding it along with his pole as we walked from the car to the pier." Mr. Davis drew in a breath. "We're parked right there." He nodded toward a late model, dark blue crossover SUV in a parking space a few feet away. "I didn't see the need to walk with him."

Chalissa visually measured the distance from the chairs to the SUV —about fifty feet.

"He's nearly eight, and we've been working on him doing things by himself because..."

"A boy needs his independence," she finished the thought for him.

"Yeah," he agreed.

"But you watched him all the way to the car?"

"Yes. I saw him pick up the lure—it was on the ground right by the back passenger-side door, where he must have dropped it as he got out of the car."

Mr. Davis closed his eyes briefly, pain etched into the lines of his face. "Then I got a text. I only looked away for a few seconds."

"From your wife?" As soon as the words left her mouth, Chalissa wanted them back. At least her voice had sounded brisk, professional, and not inquiring.

"No." Mr. Davis looked away. "My wife, Sam's mom, died when he was a baby."

She winced for pouring more pain on an already-painful situation. "I'm so sorry."

"Thank you." He squared his shoulders. "I read the text, and when I looked up again, Sam wasn't there."

"You didn't answer the text?"

"It was spam." His gaze locked with hers. "You don't think it was sent on purpose to distract me from Sam? Let me show you." He pulled out his phone and brought up the text. As she read the short message, he continued, "It was something about my credit card account, but my credit card company doesn't communicate that sort of information by text."

"Thanks." The text had standard spam language, but given the timing, she noted the sender's number just in case. "Where have you looked for your son?"

"All around here."

"Excuse me?" An older man wearing the brown uniform of a park employee approached them. "Are you the father with the missing boy?"

"Yes, I'm Titus Davis."

"Nathan Wiltshire." He turned toward Chalissa. "And you are?"

"Chalissa Manning, U.S. Marshal." She shook his hand. "I left my official ID in my vehicle, but while running on the trail, I heard Mr. Davis calling for help." She held up her phone. "I've taken down all the pertinent information about what happened, including a description of Sam, age seven. If you'll give me your contact info, I'll send it to you to disperse to the park employees."

Mr. Wiltshire rattled off his phone number. "That will make things easier."

"I have to look for Sam," Mr. Davis said. "I can't just stand around doing nothing."

The park employee shook his head. "It's best if you stay here, in case Sam comes back on his own." He held up a hand as Mr. Davis opened his mouth. "I know how difficult a request that is. If it were my son, I'd want to be searching the grounds too. But it really is best if you leave the search to park workers and the police."

"You've called the police?" Chalissa asked.

"Yes, as soon as I heard the boy was missing." A shadow passed over Mr. Wiltshire's face. "Another Northern Virginia park had a similar incident about five years ago and the Northern Virginia Park Authority management made the decision that any time a child was reported missing on park grounds, the police would be brought in immediately."

Chalissa heard the sorrow behind the words and hoped Mr. Davis hadn't picked up on the inflection. That incident probably hadn't turned out well, but there was no need for Mr. Davis to start imagining anything darker than he already was.

The other man extended his hand to Mr. Davis, who shook it impatiently. "Hang tight. I'll keep you updated. I'm going to make sure everyone is looking for your son."

As the park employee walked away, Chalissa turned back to the father. "Is there anyone I can call for you?"

"Call?" His eyes widened. "No, I'll take care of it. Excuse me."

She watched him move toward his vehicle, fear and concern slumping his shoulders. The knot in the pit of her stomach tightened even more. She could relate to how terrified Mr. Davis must be feeling, how helpless, particularly since his missing son had special needs. For a moment, the temptation to cry out to God to save Sam, to not let Brandon's fate befall him, overwhelmed her. But personal experience had confirmed God didn't answer her prayers.

HANGING ONTO HIS CONTROL BY A WIRE AS THIN AS THE FISHING LINE on his rod, Titus leaned his back against the rear bumper of his SUV. Tremors shook his hands and it took him three tries to select the right number to call.

"Mac here."

U.S. Marshal James "Mac" MacIntire's familiar, crisp greeting nearly made Titus cry out in relief. "It's Titus. Sam is missing."

"What happened?"

Titus quickly recounted the events of the morning. "The park has started a search and called in the local police."

"Could Sam be playing a game?" Mac's question irritated Titus.

His son knew better than to play a game like this, but he bit his tongue to prevent himself from taking out his fear on Mac. "I don't think so. Sam usually follows the rules."

"Did you and Sam run into anyone you know at the park?"

"No." Titus could hear the fear in his own voice. "With the trial coming up in a couple of weeks..." He let the thought trail off, knowing Mac would understand.

"You did the right thing in calling me."

"Mr. Davis?"

Titus raised his head and met the direct gaze of Chalissa Manning, a serious expression stamped on her face. "Hold a minute, Mac." He put the phone down.

"The police have arrived." She pointed over her shoulder to where a trio of officers made their way through the crowd toward him. "I'll brief them while you finish your call."

"Thanks." Titus put the phone back to his ear as she moved toward the officers. "The police are here."

"Good. Who was that you were talking to just now?"

"Chalissa Manning. A jogger on the path who heard me shouting for Sam. She offered to help. She said she was a U.S. Marshal, but she didn't have any identification on her." The tranquility and compassion in her eyes as she questioned him had done much to calm him during those first few moments of panic at the realization Sam was missing.

"You didn't say anything?" Mac's question stung.

"Of course not," Titus snapped. "I merely gave her the information necessary to find Sam." He lowered his voice, his gaze seeking out Chalissa, where she stood talking to the police. "I certainly didn't blurt out I'm in witness protection."

"Good. We do have a new inspector who arrived last week from the St. Louis office, but I haven't met him or her yet." Mac cleared his throat. "Unfortunately, I'm four hours away in southwestern Virginia, but let me check with the office on the new inspector. If it is this Chalissa Manning, I'll call and brief her, so she can take over as your point-of-contact during the search."

"Okay."

"For now, follow protocol and don't say a word to anyone about your being in WITSEC."

"Got it." Titus ended the call as Chalissa waved him over. As he walked toward the group of officers, the same prayer looped over and over in his mind. *Please God, keep Sam safe. Don't let him be hurt because of me.*

# CHAPTER 2

"He was wearing sneakers, jeans, and a bright orange fishing vest over a long-sleeved blue T-shirt." Titus craned his neck to keep an eye on Chalissa Manning, who had stepped away to answer a phone call, leaving him to answer the same set of questions she'd asked. For some reason, her presence calmed him.

"Is there anything else we need to know, Mr. Davis?" Officer Caleb Lawrence looked up from his notebook.

"He's autistic." Titus tucked his hands under his arms to stop them from shaking. Talking about his son to the police made his absence all the more frightening. He hated labeling Sam, but he hoped revealing his son's condition would both spur the police to accelerate their search and assist them in approaching Sam when he was found. *When.* He couldn't think about the alternative.

"My son is what they call 'high functioning.' His autism mostly manifests in his interpersonal relationships in that he misses social cues and has trouble interacting with his peers. He's much better talking to adults." His voice threatened to crack as the weight of fear for Sam pressed down on him. "He also has a big heart and is very trusting. If someone asked him for help, well, he'd give it without a second thought."

The police officer jotted something down. "I'll make sure the officers know about his diagnosis. We're circulating Sam's photo and description of what he was wearing. The park employees are assisting our officers in a search of the grounds. We will do everything possible to facilitate a good outcome."

A good outcome. Law enforcement speak for finding his son safe and unharmed. But they didn't know what Titus did—that someone wanted to stop Titus from testifying in a trial set to start in two weeks. And that someone had proved adept at silencing witnesses. Whether that included harming children, Titus prayed he wouldn't find out. Officer Lawrence made his way to the knot of cops standing at the mouth of the parking lot.

"Mr. Davis?" Chalissa touched his arm. "Mac briefed me on your situation."

"So you know," he dropped his voice and dipped his head closer to hers to avoid being overheard by the gathering crowd milling around them, "I'm, uh, in the program?"

As word spread about a missing child, park goers began to congregate near the boat launch, asking how they could help with the search.

"Yes." She met his gaze, her brown eyes filled with concern. "Mac said your trial begins in two weeks. You haven't seen anyone following you lately?"

Titus shook his head. "No, everything seems like it's the same."

"For now, we'll keep your involvement with the program to ourselves. No need to muddy the water with speculation or blow your cover." She consulted her phone. "Sam's been missing for forty minutes. There's a very good chance he's somewhere safe in the park. Did you see someone you knew at the park?"

"No." Then a snippet of conversation pushed its way to the surface of his mind. "Wait a minute. When we passed the parking lot by the information building, Sam did say something about seeing one of his classmates, Vanessa Jennings, and her mom."

"Is that the lot off to the right as you enter the park from Ox Road?"

"Yes." Titus drew in a breath to steady himself, but his pulse refused to slow down. Every minute Sam was missing twisted his gut into tighter knots.

"Is he friends with Vanessa?" At his affirmation, she said, "Is it possible he went to talk to her?"

"That doesn't sound like Sam." Sam knew the rules, but lately, he'd been pushing back against some of the strictures Titus had put in place. "Sam's teacher has sent home a couple of notes recently about the two of them talking too much in class."

"Do you have contact info for Vanessa' parents?"

Titus pulled out his phone to find Barbara Jennings. "I should have it here." He paused, raising his eyes to Chalissa's face. "Do you really think he could be with Vanessa?"

"It's possible."

"I found her number." He tapped the screen, then lifted the phone to his ear.

"Can you put it on speaker?"

With a nod, he touched the screen again and the sound of a phone ringing pierced the air.

"Well, hello, Titus," a woman said, her tone a bit breathless. "I was beginning to think you were ignoring me."

"Hi, Barbara." His cheeks warmed with the flirty response. "Have you seen my—"

"I've been meaning to call you," Barbara spoke at the same time. "Vanessa wanted to invite Sam to go to the Baltimore Aquarium for her birthday. It's one of those spend-the-night-with-the-fish type things, and it's—"

"I'm sure Sam would enjoy that," Titus cut in. "Is Sam with Vanessa now?"

The urgency in his voice must have alerted Barbara this wasn't a social call. "Yes, of course they're together. They're riding the mini-train. You didn't know? I'm so sorry. Sam said you told him he could ride the train with Vanessa, then go fishing."

Titus sagged against a nearby vehicle, relief turning his bones to cooked spaghetti. "Can you see him?"

"The train is pulling into the station now. Yes, he's there with Vanessa."

"Please wait at the station with Sam until I get there," Titus requested. "I'll be a few minutes because I'll need to let the park and police know he's been found."

"I'm so sorry," Barbara repeated. "If I'd had any inkling you didn't know where Sam was, I'd have called you immediately." The conciliation in Barbara's voice barely registered.

"Just stay with him at the train station until I get there," he reiterated.

"Absolutely."

Titus said goodbye and clicked off, closing his eyes briefly to send a short prayer of thanks for his son's safety.

Chalissa nudged his arm with her elbow. "Go to your son."

He tried to form a thank you, but the ebbing panic mixed with the release of tension held his tongue hostage.

"Go. I'll let the officers and park employees know Sam's been found."

With a nod of thanks, Titus pushed off from the vehicle and jogged toward the train station and his son.

CHALISSA THANKED THE OFFICER IN CHARGE OF THE SEARCH, THE relief on his face mirroring her own. Personal experience had taught her not to take good outcomes like this one for granted. She found a secluded spot and punched in Mac's number to bring the Marshal up-to-date.

"Mac here."

"It's Chalissa Manning. Sam's safe and sound."

"Thank goodness. What happened?"

She quickly recapped the events. "Because we found Sam relatively quickly, we didn't have to inform law enforcement of Mr. Davis's inclusion in the program, so his cover is still intact."

"That's even better news."

"I think so too. I'll check in with Mr. Davis to make sure he doesn't have any additional concerns and start the paperwork at the office."

"That can wait until Monday—no need to monopolize your entire weekend with paperwork."

"I'd rather get it underway now while it's fresh in my mind." While Chalissa appreciated Mac's offer, she had nothing else going on, so she might as well work. But she would keep that truth to herself. No need to let a colleague know about her pathetic social life.

"Suit yourself. See you Monday, and thanks again for handling the situation on the ground."

"No problem." Chalissa ended the call, then walked down the pier to gather the blue camping chairs Mr. Davis had set up for fishing. She deposited the chairs by the rear bumper of the Davis vehicle, then retrieved the fishing gear Mr. Davis had left behind. Positioning herself by the vehicle, she waited for Mr. Davis and Sam to return.

A few minutes later, Mr. Davis came into view holding the hand of a sandy-haired boy with glasses. The child skipped along beside his dad, apparently unaffected by the trauma of the morning. As the pair approached the SUV, Mr. Davis wore an expression of relief mingled with love as he cocked his head toward Sam.

When Sam spotted Chalissa, he halted. "You're standing by our car."

"You're right," Chalissa replied.

"Ms. Manning, this is my son, Sam. Sam, Ms. Manning helped me when I was looking for you." Mr. Davis kept his hand on his son's shoulder.

"Hi!" Sam's eyes sparkled. "The train's whistle blew five times!"

"Hello, Sam." Chalissa smiled. "It sounds like you enjoyed your train ride."

"Yeah, it was a lot of fun." Sam sidled closer to his father. "We went around the track two times."

Mr. Davis pointed to the chairs and fishing rods. "Did you bring these up from the pier?"

She nodded. "Figured you'd probably want to leave after the morning's events."

"That was thoughtful of you." Mr. Davis turned to his son. "Sam, please get into the car while I load the gear into the back."

"We're not going fishing today?" Sam's lower lip jutted out.

Mr. Davis laid a hand on Sam's shoulder. "No, I told you. You went off with Vanessa without permission. So we're going home now."

Sam stamped his foot. "I wanna go fishing!"

"I asked you to get into the car." Mr. Davis threw an apologetic look to Chalissa, then refocused his attention on Sam.

"No!" Sam's voice rose. "I wanna fish! Fish! Fish! Fish!"

His loud cries drew the attention of passersby, but Mr. Davis's attention didn't stray from his son, whose face grew red. When Mr. Davis lifted the boy by placing his hands under Sam's armpits, Sam abandoned words entirely and screamed.

Several people stopped to stare as he carried the squirming, yelling child around to the passenger side of the vehicle.

"Nothing to see here, folks." Chalissa made a shooing gesture with her hands to the gawkers, who thankfully took the hint and moved on.

She glanced over her shoulder to see how Mr. Davis was faring. Sam's cries had settled down to whimpers as his father buckled him into his car seat.

Chalissa tested the hatch release and found it unlocked. She quickly loaded the chairs and fishing gear inside and closed the tailgate nearly in sync with Mr. Davis shutting Sam's door.

He joined her at the rear bumper, the lines on his face more pronounced. "Sorry about that."

"No need to apologize." Sam's behavior didn't faze her at all. Brandon had acted far worse when disappointed. "You need to get going, but I wanted to let you know I informed Mac about the outcome, and the police have alerted the volunteers and park employees involved in the search."

"Good." Mr. Davis swallowed hard. "I would like to thank them for their help."

"I got the name and contact information for Nathan Wiltshire, the park employee we spoke to initially, and Captain Daniel Parker, who coordinated the search. I can send you their info if you'd like."

"Yes, please. You can text it to my cell." He gave her his number. "I can't thank you enough for your assistance today."

"I was happy to help." She paused, then added, "You were great with Sam just now."

He smiled, the gesture erasing the lines of tension in his face. Her heart thudded in her chest as her eyes locked with his. For a moment, she thought he might say something more, but then the moment passed and he nodded once before moving to the driver's side of the SUV.

As Chalissa walked briskly to retrieve her car in another parking lot, the image of his handsome face filled her mind. She could admire his good looks all she wanted to, but given his status as a witness and hers as an inspector, admiration from afar was all she could hope for.

# CHAPTER 3

C halissa refilled her mug, dumping in two sugar packets and a healthy dollop of half-and-half. She usually didn't take much sugar in her coffee, but this particular Monday morning, she needed a little extra boost.

"Chalissa?" Janette Turner poked her head into the break room. "You're needed in Conference Room B, pronto."

"Thanks, I'll be there as soon as I grab a notebook." Chalissa hurried to her cubicle, careful not to slosh her coffee. An unscheduled meeting was never a good sign. Entering the smaller of the two conference rooms, she recognized Mac from her weekend debriefing after the Davis incident and their boss, U.S. Marshal Kristine Wong, but not the two visitors, who both wore navy suits and somber expressions.

"Chalissa, thanks for joining us," Wong said. "You know Inspector MacIntire."

She nodded to Mac as she set her mug on the conference table and slid into the chair beside him.

"This is Federal Prosecutor Leela Burgess and Federal Prosecutor Graham Powell from North Carolina," Wong continued the introductions as Chalissa half stood to shake each attorney's hand. "This is the newest member of our team, Inspector Chalissa Manning."

"Inspector MacIntire related the events of the weekend in regard to Mr. Davis already. Ms. Burgess and Mr. Powell are here to prep Mr. Davis for the upcoming trial. " Wong leaned back in her chair at the head of the table, her gaze on Chalissa. "But since Mac will soon be on paternity leave, he suggested you step in as Mr. Davis's handler in the interim."

"Happy to help." Chalissa arranged her notebook and uncapped her pen, then addressed the U.S. attorneys. "I assume meeting here to go over Mr. Davis's testimony would work for you?"

Ms. Burgess held up her hand. "Before we go any further, there's something else that needs to be discussed." She exchanged a look with her colleague, who opened his laptop and hit a few keys. "It's recently come to our attention that Mr. Davis wasn't as forthcoming with his involvement in Miller Construction as he indicated in his previous statements."

Chalissa frowned. This didn't sound good.

"What do you mean?" Mac asked, his voice measured, but a slight tightening of his jaw indicated he wasn't pleased with the direction of the conversation.

"I mean Mr. Davis lied to us," Ms. Burgess snapped. "He wasn't an innocent bystander who lucked into figuring out the company was laundering money for the Yanovich family—he was an active participant."

"Now, wait a minute." Mac straightened in his chair. "That's quite an accusation. Our witness provided enough documentation to show exactly what was happening at Miller Construction. He named names, which wasn't easy, considering he had a young son to think about. You people have had six years to build this case, and this is the first anyone has even hinted Mr. Davis was directly involved in money laundering."

"Inspector," Ms. Burgess said, "Mr. Davis's testimony is crucial to proving our case against Miller Construction and key members of the Yanovich family, but my key witness can't lie on the stand."

"I've known Davis for three years," Mac said. "He's so honest, he makes Boy Scouts look crooked."

Chalissa agreed with Mac's assessment. The man appeared to be an upright citizen who loved his son. However, she also knew love didn't mean one chose the right thing to do—not when fear for the safety of one's family loomed large.

"That's what he wanted you to think—wanted everyone to think," Ms. Burgess replied. "But we have new evidence that throws into question everything Mr. Davis said relating to this case."

"It's rather convenient, this new 'evidence,'" Mac used his fingers to make air quotes, "has come to light now with the trial starting in less than two weeks."

"Our office considered the timing, but that was before we examined the evidence." Ms. Burgess waved a hand at Mr. Powell. "Play the video."

"Good morning, Mac," Titus greeted the Marshal at the reception desk. He'd arrived as instructed by Mac for trial prep with the federal prosecutors in charge of the case. "Only a few more days until Cindy has the baby, right?"

"Yeah, we can't wait. Speaking of the baby's arrival, Deputy Wong assigned Chalissa Manning to be your handler while I'm out on paternity leave." Mac led the way down the hall, stopping outside of Conference Room B. He glanced at Titus. "Listen, I—"

Deputy Wong opened the conference room door. "Mr. Davis? They're ready for you."

Mac gestured for Titus to precede him into the room. Chalissa looked up as he entered, while two strangers sat opposite her, their heads huddled together. Titus took a seat beside Chalissa with Mac to his right. After introducing Ms. Burgess and Mr. Powell to Titus, Deputy Wong excused herself.

"We'll get started in just a few minutes," Ms. Burgess said, then conferred with Mr. Powell in whispers while Mac responded to a text message on his phone.

"How's Sam doing after Saturday's ordeal?" Chalissa said softly.

"He's okay. Still disappointed about not fishing." Titus resisted the urge to explain how Sam wouldn't let go of the missed outing. His thoughts traveled back to the park. Sam had talked nonstop the remainder of Saturday and all day Sunday about wanting to catch some fish. Titus had managed not to respond beyond a "hmmm" to Sam's comments, per instructions from his son's occupational therapist. According to the counselor, the best way to help the boy move away from his fixation was to not engage him when he became obsessive over something.

"There's always next Saturday," she said.

Titus frowned, not sure what he'd missed.

"For fishing with Sam," Chalissa filled in for him.

"Right, sorry, my mind's a little scattered this morning," he said.

"No worries." She offered a quick smile as her phone buzzed. "Sorry, need to answer this." Chalissa bent over her phone, leaving him alone with his thoughts.

He started to drum his fingers on the table to have something to do with his hands, then stopped. The room hummed as if it were a violin objecting to the bow being dragged across its too-tight strings.

When Titus first approached a lawyer friend about the irregularities he'd discovered in Miller Construction's books, he'd known there was no going back. A series of subsequent meetings with the lawyer and FBI agents confirmed his suspicions. The company, which built roads, sidewalks, and driveways for new housing developments, had been a small family-owned business for years until the current owner had expanded too quickly. The company's management team had decided one way to keep afloat during the Great Recession would be to accept "help" from an outfit with connections to a tentacle of the Yanovich family.

Over the course of four nerve-racking months—which began shortly after his wife lost her battle with ovarian cancer—Titus dutifully gathered the hard evidence, then entered the federal Witness Protection Program with his son. Six years had passed while attorneys for the government and defendants wrangled over whatever it was lawyers threw at each other ahead of a trial. During that time, Titus had been occasionally contacted to provide additional information, but mostly, the past seventy-two months had been a waiting game. In fact, until last month, when the trial date had finally been set, he'd managed to push thoughts of his former life behind him.

"Thank you for your patience," Ms. Burgess said.

Titus yanked his thoughts from the past to listen as the lead federal prosecutor brought the meeting to order.

"Mr. Davis, as you know, the trial is set to begin in two weeks," Ms. Burgess said.

Titus's stomach clenched at the undertone in her voice, making him regret the eggs and bacon he'd eaten with Sam at breakfast. He nodded, trying to project a countenance of ease.

Ms. Burgess stared straight at Titus, her eyes as hard as the Virginia clay Sam dug up in their backyard when pretending to excavate dinosaur bones. "A new piece of evidence has come to light, one that has the potential to derail years of hard work both by our office and the FBI."

Titus flicked a glance to Mac, who didn't meet his gaze. A quick look at Chalissa found her studying him with a closed expression.

"What is it?" Titus asked when no one else spoke.

"A video." Ms. Burgess motioned to her colleague, who clicked the mousepad on his open laptop. The room's large projector screen came to life and a sense of foreboding steamrolled across his chest. Mac dimmed the lights as a slightly fuzzy video began to play.

At first, Titus couldn't decipher the location, given the tight shot of the camera, which appeared rectangular, like from a cell phone.

The audio was indistinct, but as the camera inched closer, two figures talking at a small conference table came into view. One was the CEO of Miller Construction, John Miller, and the other was himself.

The camera stopped a few feet away, shook slightly, then stabilized as if the person holding it had propped it up. Folders and papers nearly covered the entire top of the round table.

"That's all, Janet. You can go," John said.

The woman crossed in front of the camera, then exited the screen.

Mr. Powell hit the pause button. "We've verified the person leaving as Janet Devonshire, Miller's long-time assistant."

Titus said, "Janet retired from the company shortly before I left."

Again, the lawyers exchanged a quick look. "That's correct. She died a few months ago."

"She's dead?" His heart began to pump more vigorously. "How?"

"Breast cancer. She'd beaten it in her forties but it came back. This time, she lost the battle," Mac said. "Since she's on the witness list, we confirmed cancer was in fact the cause of death."

That reassurance only marginally calmed Titus. Janet had always been kind to him, especially after Eve's death. She brought him casseroles once a week for months after Eve's funeral and always asked how he and Sam were doing. "Was she going to testify against Miller Construction?"

"She was willing to testify, but insisted Miller had no idea what was happening in the company," Ms. Burgess said. "Janet believed others might have been complicit but Miller's hands were clean. We suspect she might have been in love with Miller. After all, she doted on him hand and foot and never married. She only retired because arthritis in her hands made it virtually impossible to handle office duties."

Titus recalled the tears in Janet's eyes during her retirement party. She'd worked for Miller Construction for more than half a century, starting out as a young girl straight out of high school.

"Let's continue." Mr. Powell restarted the video.

For a couple of minutes, nothing happened beyond Titus and John discussing the company budget. As the video played, Titus racked his brain to try to place it during his time at the company. His white shirt, tie, and slacks gave him no clue—that had been his standard "uniform" as the company accountant.

"Is that all? I tee off at two o'clock," John said.

On the video, Titus said, "There is one more thing." He rummaged through folders on the jobsite conference table, then plucked one out of a stack. "I'd like you to take a look at these invoices." He handed the document to the CEO, who appeared to read it.

"What about it?" John tossed the invoice onto the table.

"It's a duplicate." Titus opened another folder and showed the CEO another file. "See? We already paid for this exact same service."

"We're being double-billed?" John said.

"No, we're paying for the same thing to two different companies." He shuffled through the folders and laid two invoices side by side. "Here we paid $12,000 to Reedy Cement Company on April 3, and here we paid $12,000 to Reeding USA Cement Company on April 8."

"That's two separate companies and dates. How are those similar?" John asked.

"If you look at the April 8 invoice, you'll see that it's been over-written—the three became an eight. The 'y' was overwritten with 'ing,' and 'USA' was inserted before Cement to create the impression of a new invoice." Titus tapped the folder in the video. "I went back and spot-checked other large invoices, and this type of thing happens on a regular basis. We'll have a legitimate invoice come through, then a few days or weeks later, a second invoice for the exact same service or product with the altered dates and company name."

In the conference room, the federal prosecutors leaned toward the TV screen as if in anticipation of what was to come. Apprehension rolled over Titus like the treaded tires of a giant excavator, crushing the breath from his body as his chest tightened. Something was coming, something that wouldn't be good for him.

"I see." John tapped the papers. "What should we do?"

The question hung in the air as if supported by the wings of a circling hawk.

On-screen, Titus shifted out of the frame. "Continue doing business as before," he said, his voice sounding hollow.

The video abruptly ended with a flicker of light.

# CHAPTER 4

Having watched the video before Mr. Davis's arrival, Chalissa snuck glances at him beside her during the viewing. The stiffness of his shoulders and the set of his jaw told her more than words how the video was affecting him. A few times, she had to stop herself from reaching over and touching his arm to reassure him he had a friend in the room. No matter how she longed to be a friend to this devoted father, she had to remain focused as his temporary WITSEC inspector and keep things professional. Not allowing herself to think of him as *Titus* was one way to accomplish that. Yet distancing herself was proving more difficult than anticipated.

In her four years with the Marshal service, she'd never been tempted to cross the line between private and professional with her witnesses. However, in the space of a few days, it became more clear to her why some of her fellow agents got wrapped up in personal relationships with those they were sworn to protect.

When the screen went blank at the video's end, Titus—*Mr. Davis* —didn't move. Mac returned the lights to full brightness.

Ms. Burgess tapped her pen on the yellow legal pad in front of her. "Mr. Davis, it appears that you have not been forthcoming with us about your involvement in the money laundering scheme allegedly run by Miller and other management personnel. In fact," she flipped through a thick folder, "you stated during your initial deposition you had nothing to do with the double invoicing."

"That's right," Titus said, his voice cracking with strong emotion.

Chalissa metaphorically threw up her hands at her inability to think about the man beside her as Mr. Davis. In truth, he had ceased being Mr. Davis to her after the happy outcome to his missing son on Saturday.

"I noticed the discrepancies and brought it to John's attention eight months before I came to you," Titus said. "Ms. Burgess, I had nothing to do with the double invoicing and the other abnormalities I discovered at Miller Construction. I did *not* lie during my deposition. Everything I told your office when I entered Witness Protection is true."

"I can't help you if you are uncooperative with us," Ms. Burgess said as if Titus hadn't spoken. "On this video, you clearly ask to be cut in on the deal."

Titus opened his mouth, but the federal prosecutor held up her hand. She leaned forward across the table and narrowed her eyes. "You wanted to receive money in exchange for overlooking the duplicate billing. There's no other way to interpret your last statement."

Chalissa felt the anger rolling off Titus like waves pounding the surf. She jumped in before he could respond, "Let's not speculate about what appears to happen on-screen. I'd like more information about the video itself."

Mac turned to Titus. "Mr. Davis, why don't you and I get a cup of coffee?"

For a moment, Chalissa thought Titus wouldn't leave, but he rose and left, Mac right behind him. Once the door closed behind them, Mr. Powell said, "Our forensics team identified the video as taken from a cell phone."

"Where did you get this video?" Chalissa asked.

"From Ms. Devonshire's estate," Mr. Powell said.

Chalissa jotted that down. "Was it a file on her phone or on her computer?"

Mr. Powell frowned, his gaze directed at his computer screen. "The email doesn't say."

"Who sent it to your office?" Chalissa continued her questions.

"The estate's attorney," Mr. Powell said. "A Mr. Wayne Treeman."

"Were you able to verify this video was taken by Ms. Devonshire? And that it hadn't been tampered with in any way?" Chalissa pressed.

"Our tech department said it appears genuine," Mr. Powell replied, but Chalissa detected annoyance in his tone.

Chalissa asked some more questions related to the video but she couldn't get any more definitive answers. The timing of the video surfacing two weeks before the trial smacked of something underhanded by the defendant. While the prosecutors focused on the evidence as it related to their case, Chalissa worried about what it might mean for the safety of her witness. If the video was a fake—and even after knowing Titus for such a short time, she believed his statement that he hadn't taken any money—that meant someone was stepping up harassment against Titus. Which meant she needed to be on her guard and near Titus more until he testified.

Mac and Titus returned, each holding a mug. Titus returned to his seat next to Chalissa.

Titus put down his cup, his tension palpable. Before anyone else spoke, he spat out, his anger barely leashed, "You people went through my financials with a fine-tooth comb when I came forward. If—and that's a big *if*—I had taken a bribe, where's the money? I accounted for every penny I ever earned, received, or paid during my entire tenure with Miller Construction."

Ms. Burgess pursed her lips. "For the record, we are re-examining your financial history." She drilled Titus with a hard look, one Chalissa imagined worked well when questioning opposing witnesses on the stand. "Rest assured, Mr. Davis, if there's a money trail to follow, we will find it."

"I did not take anything!" Titus raked his hand through his hair. "And I certainly did not help Miller Construction launder money."

"What happens now?" Mac cut in, his voice measured.

"We don't have enough to prove beyond a reasonable doubt that Mr. Davis was involved in the very crime to which he has agreed to testify," Ms. Burgess said crisply. "We will be in touch as the investigation progresses." She stood, gathering folders as her colleague did the same. "And when we do find the evidence, your contract with the U.S. Marshals will be null and void."

With that, the pair left the conference room. As the door closed behind the attorneys, Mac turned to Titus. "I know this seems—"

"Like I'm a liar?" Titus shot out of his chair and paced on the other side of the conference table. "Like I took bribes and helped launder money for the Yanovich family? This is a setup. That video must have been altered or faked in some way. The trial starts in two weeks, and they're trying to discredit my testimony." He gripped the back of a chair. "What if they find more trumped-up evidence pointing to my guilt? They'll kick me out of the program. If that happens, Sam and I will be dead long before the trial begins."

Chalissa bit her lip to avoid saying death was the least of his worries if he was forced out of the program.

Mac wasn't one to pull punches. "That's not all that would happen."

"What do you mean?" Titus's knuckles turned white from his grip on the chair back.

Chalissa answered for Mac. "If they find enough evidence, they'll move you from witness for the prosecution to defendant."

The color drained from Titus's face so fast Chalissa half rose from her chair in anticipation of his fainting. But the man across from her stayed upright.

"I could go to jail?" The words spoken in a whisper carried with them the weight of the world.

"Let's not get ahead of ourselves." Mac stood and moved to put his hand on Titus's shoulder. "We'll get to the bottom of this. I'll bring Chalissa up to speed on your case, and we'll see what can be done."

Titus's lips twitched. "Okay."

"For now, go about your normal routine, and we'll be in touch." Mac guided him to the door. "I'll walk you out."

On Chalissa's return to her cubicle, she stopped to ask the unit admin if he could pull the Davis file for her. If she was going to figure out who was setting up her witness, she had to start with what exactly he had told the prosecutors to enter the program and who would want him discredited—or dead.

TITUS CLICKED TO CHANGE THE BACKGROUND COLOR ON A WEBSITE HE was designing for a snack subscription start-up. The bright gold color suggested by the client definitely didn't work with the font and photos. Maybe a more burnished tone of gold would bring the page to life.

As he fiddled with the color scheme, the video from yesterday's meeting replayed in the back of his mind. Someone must have tampered with the video to make it seem like he was asking for a cut of the action. He had a million questions to ask, none of which he could pursue without endangering his status as a witness. Even searching for information online could reveal his location. If he'd learned anything in his web design courses, it was how easily one could use websites to gather intel on browsing history and user interaction.

"Titus, you coming?"

Titus swiveled around to see one of his colleagues, Yvette Single-ton, standing at his cubicle entrance. "Yeah, sorry, deep in thought." Her words registered more fully. "Where am I going?"

She raised her eyebrows. "To the staff meeting."

"It's two thirty already?" He rose, grabbing a pad and pen.

"Yep." Yvette moved down the hallway toward the large conference room.

As he hurried to catch up, Titus tried to bring his mind around to work. The office had been buzzing with rumors of a merger with another company, and the potential for layoffs had everyone on edge these past few weeks.

Yvette squeezed into the last available chair, leaving Titus to find a space along the back wall. A few other workers joined him as the president of Spider Web Design called the meeting to order.

"I have very good news." Jamie Hewson beamed at the group.

Rumors had circulated about the company's shaky financial footing, but he hadn't paid close attention. As a lowly website designer with only three years' seniority, he kept his head down and did his job. His being in witness protection meant he needed to keep a low profile, so staying out of office politics made sense.

"As some of you are aware, we've lost a few key accounts lately," Hewson continued. "However, most of those accounts left because they wanted a website company that didn't only build a great website, but one that helped them obtain clients through marketing efforts tied to the website. That's why I'm pleased to announce, effective immediately, we are merging with All For You Marketing to create a new company, Spider Web Design & Marketing."

Someone started clapping and Titus joined the other employees in the round of applause.

"There are still a lot of details to work out, but for now, we will be staying in this office space at least until our lease expires in three years," Hewson said.

"Will there be layoffs?" a man in the far corner called out.

"We plan to take a hard look at our personnel and see where we might need to trim," Hewson said.

As the crowd began to murmur, Titus looked down at the high-traffic carpet to avoid being pulled into the banter. Up till now he hadn't socialized much with his coworkers and he wanted to keep his low profile in the office.

Hewson spoke over the crowd. "Those who are part of the layoff *will receive* a generous severance package." The volume in the room simmered as Hewson continued. "We will also provide assistance in finding another job."

"When will we know?" a woman said.

"I'm not sure. I know you have more questions, but that's all I can say for now."

Titus slipped out of the room as soon as he could, not wanting to get sucked into discussions about whose job would be axed. His only goal was to get through the rest of the day so he could concentrate his full attention on how to counter the fake evidence aimed at bringing him down.

Twenty minutes later, he was immersed in the redesign of a chiropractor's website when someone tapped on the opening to his partition. When he glanced up, Dwayne Redman leaned over the chest-high wall, his eyes large behind thick lenses.

"When do you think they will start the purge?" Dwayne asked, his fingers playing a staccato rhythm on the top of the wall. "And why did Jamie say it was good news when people will lose their jobs?"

"Mr. Hewson said he didn't know. And you're right—that wasn't very good news, was it?" Titus resisted the urge to turn back to his computer. With everything else going on, he had found it difficult to concentrate on his work and he didn't want to get behind on this project. Dwayne had an abrasive personality that rubbed most people the wrong way, but Titus had seen much of his son in the awkward man and had chosen to look past his quirks. Sam displayed some of the same directness, the same missing of social cues, and that had made Titus more willing to listen to Dwayne.

"Do you think it will be by seniority?" Dwayne continued to drum his fingers to music only he could hear, the movement vibrating the wall and fluttering the sticky notes Titus had thumbtacked to the surface.

"Perhaps. If so, my job would be toast. I'm one of the most recent hires in the graphics design department."

"Oh, no. You're really good. And people like you." Dwayne nodded his head as if to emphasize his point. "I'm sure your job will be safe."

Titus looked more closely at Dwayne, picking up on the anxiety behind the man's words. "You're worried about your job."

"Yes." Dwayne stopped tapping. "People don't like me. I make them uncomfortable."

Reassuring the other man the statement wasn't true wouldn't work. Titus had learned early on that Dwayne took any attempt at soothing his feelings as pity. Instead, he switched topics. "You've been here how long?"

"Twenty-seven years next month." Dwayne straightened. "I gave Jamie the idea to start this company."

Titus hadn't heard that version of the company's origins, which differed from the official one. "I didn't know that."

"I knocked off his papers at a coffee shop and saw some code for a website. I liked building websites on my own, and I pointed out a flaw in the HTML code." Dwayne smiled, then sobered quickly. "Jamie and I worked on the business plan together, but he's better with people, and we agreed he would be the public face and I would do the design work. But that was a long time ago. He hardly ever talks to me these days."

"I'm sure it's just because he's been so busy with the merger."

"You might be right." The fierce look on the other man's face reminded Titus of a cornered animal. "He'd better not try to push me out. I'm a part owner in this firm and he owes me."

Titus's desk phone rang.

"I've got to go." Dwayne pointed to the still-ringing phone. "You'd better get that."

Dwayne's tension, evident in the stiffness of his body as he walked away, bothered Titus. Maybe he'd ask Dwayne to lunch later this week to see if he could help his colleague adjust to the company changes. Titus picked up the handset. "Hello, this is Titus Davis."

"It's Chalissa Manning."

At the sound of her voice, his pulse jumped and his mood lightened. Without thinking, he said, "Inspector Manning, this is a pleasant surprise."

For a few seconds, she didn't respond. Great, he must have put more warmth into the greeting than he'd intended and crossed some invisible line between Marshal and witness.

"Mr. Davis, we need to talk." Her clipped words doused whatever tender emotion had temporarily taken over his senses.

Titus straightened in his chair. "Okay. What about?"

"Not over the phone. Can you meet me later today?"

"Let me check." He pulled up his calendar. "Tonight Sam has soccer practice at six."

"Can you talk during his practice?"

"Sure, I'm not one of the coaches. It's at the Green Acres field in Fairfax City."

"Got it. I'll be there a little after six."

Titus replaced the receiver. Now how was he going to finish his work? Maybe thinking about the green flecks he thought he'd detected in her brown eyes would be enough of a distraction from wondering about the purpose of their meeting.

# CHAPTER 5

Chalissa Manning spotted an open parking space and squeezed her SUV between a minivan with a soccer club decal and a crossover vehicle. She hoped Titus wouldn't be too distracted by his son's soccer practice to hear what she had to tell him.

As she crossed Sideburn Road, harried moms with kids in tow passed her. Ahead, a former elementary school that now housed the city's senior center stood, with its soccer fields on the right.

Near the fields, she paused to scan the groups of parents to find Titus. It took her a few minutes before she spotted him, crouched down beside Sam. His son pushed his glasses back on his nose while waving hands as he talked to Titus. She hurried over to them, dodging pint-sized kids kicking at balls and clumps of grass with their cleats.

When she was a few feet away, she called, "Mr. Davis?"

Titus raised his head. "Ah, Ms. Manning."

"Hi, Sam." She smiled at the boy, who darted a glance in her direction.

"There you go, son."

Sam inspected his footwear, then looked at Chalissa. "Do you like my dad?"

The unusual query from the seven-year-old caught her by surprise. "We just met."

"But you could like him, couldn't you?" Sam persisted as he hopped from one foot to another.

"Sam, what's going on?" Titus laid a hand on the boy's shoulder, but the child didn't acknowledge his father.

Instead, his attention focused solely on Chalissa. "My dad's really nice."

The statement, spoken with all seriousness, tugged a smile to her lips. "I'm sure your dad is nice."

At her affirmation, Sam vigorously nodded his head, sending his sandy hair flopping onto his forehead. "He is. We always go out for ice cream after practice."

"Always?" Chalissa raised her eyebrows.

"Well, not practices, but definitely after games, especially the ones I get to play in," Sam amended. "And I bet since you're here, we could go out for ice cream tonight, even though this is just a practice, right, Dad?"

"I'm sure Ms. Manning would like to get home after a long day." Titus's attempt to rein in his son didn't faze the boy.

"Lots of women make funny eyes at him," Sam leaned closer to her. "But he doesn't like any of them. Not like he likes you."

"Oh?" In spite of herself, Sam's revelations intrigued Chalissa, especially as his chatter brought a blush to his father's cheeks. Brandon had had that same uncanny ability to decipher emotions in other people even as he struggled to relate to those feelings.

"Saaammmm," Titus tried again.

"I can tell," Sam nodded. "On Saturday, he looked at you the way I feel about Snowball."

"Snowball?" She managed to keep her eyes on Sam when she longed to gauge Titus's reaction to that bombshell.

"That's my favorite stuffed animal." Sam met her gaze directly.

"I see." Chalissa recognized that look. The yearning in his eyes for two parents created a lump in her throat. She blinked them away. She was a grown woman now. No need to cry over the child she'd once been and the dashed hopes of having a mother and father under the same roof.

A shrill whistle yanked her back into the moment.

"Round up, Sprigs!" a male coach with a clipboard shouted.

"I gotta go," Sam said, "but will you stay through the practice so we can get ice cream?"

"We'll see." Chalissa didn't want to commit more until she talked to Titus.

Sam opened his mouth as if to press her, but Titus interceded. "Sam, on the field please."

"Okay." With one more look at Chalissa, Sam scurried off to join his teammates.

"Saved by the whistle," Titus said. "I'm so sorry. Lately, Sam has been on a mission to get me to date—with the goal to get him a new mom."

Chalissa seized the opening to probe more into Titus's status. His file held the bare details of his wife's death from ovarian cancer when Sam was a year old. "I'm guessing you haven't dated much since your wife's death?"

"Kinda hard to do when I can't share my past." Titus faced the field toward the team as it huddled around two coaches.

"I see." She did understand his reluctance, but many single people in WITSEC dated.

He cleared his throat, drawing her attention back to his handsome face. If she wasn't careful, she'd join the ranks of women who "liked" him. "I'm surprised Sam talked about Snowball. My wife died when Sam was young, so he doesn't remember her at all."

Something about this man and his adorable son tugged at her heart "That must have been tough for you both." No one should grow up without a mother or a father, yet too many kids did.

"It was. If I hadn't had my faith, I don't think we would have survived." Titus didn't look away from the soccer field, now filled with dozens of players all running in different directions.

"I'm sure that was a comfort to you." His faith gave her one more excellent reason to keep their relationship strictly professional. Time to change the subject.

She pulled out her phone and keyed up a photograph. "This morning, someone left a note in a plain white envelope in the mail room at the courthouse in Winston-Salem, North Carolina."

He frowned. "The courthouse where the trial is scheduled?"

"Yes." She handed the phone to Titus, the cutout letters from a newspaper glued haphazardly on a sheet of paper already burned into her mind:

> THE FOURTH OF MAY
> WHAT A DAY
> FOR JUDGE AND JURY
> I HAVE NO FURY
> BUT LAWYERS SHAM
> BAM, BAM, BAM
> WITNESSES TOO
> BOOM, BOOM, BOOM

His eyes scanned the image quickly, then studied it more closely before giving the phone back. "Is that what I think it is?"

"If you think it is a badly written poem threatening witnesses and attorneys in a trial on May 4, then yes." She pocketed the phone and let her eyes roam over the soccer field, glad to absorb the normalcy of the moment instead of the ugliness of the threat. Kids ran, coaches yelled, and parents cheered. All the noises of a community at play. "But yours isn't the only trial scheduled to begin on May 4th. The Winston-Salem courthouse has two courtrooms. The trial you're testifying in is slated for courtroom one, while courtroom two has several motions, an estate settlement, and one pretrial hearing scheduled on that date."

"Sounds like the Yanovich trial is the only high-profile case on May 4 at the courthouse," Titus said.

"Right, which is why we're taking the threat very seriously." She turned to look at Titus. "Someone from the U.S. Marshals will be either with you or watching you closely from now on."

His jaw tightened.

"I know this will make things difficult for you, especially in light of the video, but our job is to keep you and Sam safe."

Titus didn't stop gazing in the direction of the field where his son practiced. "Sam doesn't know about any of this. He was only eighteen months old when we went into the program. But now that he's older, he's been asking more questions about our family."

"You'll have to trust us to do our job as unobtrusively as possible." The words sounded hollow to her ears, but they were the truth. The only way to ensure his safety was to stick close to him and Sam, no matter the questions it raised.

On the field, Sam joined a group of kids in dribbling drills around bright orange cones spaced in a row.

"What if we dated?" The question hung in the air between them like an invisible thread, one she wanted to pull but dared not.

Chalissa cocked her head and fixed her eyes on Titus, but he still looked straight ahead. "We can't. I'm the Marshal assigned to protect you and Sam."

Titus sent her a sideways glance. "I know that. But what if we pretended to date? For Sam's sake. It would be the easiest explanation for why you'd be hanging around the house more, one Sam would buy and not ask more questions."

"For Sam." Of course, if they were seeing each other, it would be only natural she would come around to spend time with Titus. By his own admission, Sam would be over-the-moon to see his father interested in dating a woman. Chalissa might not have experience with kids, but even she could tell the heart of a matchmaker beat within his seven-year-old body. "But wouldn't he be even more hurt when he learns we were just pretending?"

"Sam already thinks I like you." Titus crossed his arms. "I'm aware of the line we can't cross because I'm a witness and you're a Marshal, but our pretending to date would seem natural to Sam."

Spending more time with this man could prove risky to her mental and emotional well-being. "I don't want to disappoint or hurt Sam. We could keep our interactions more friendly versus romantic."

The tenseness in his shoulders eased some. "Will you do it?"

"I'll have to run it by my supervisor. We have to be extra careful about anything like this these days."

"Sure, I understand." Titus opened his mouth as if to say something, then closed it with a shake of his head.

"But in the meantime," she grinned at him, "I never turn down ice cream."

Titus smiled, the gesture doing funny things to her heart. "Have you been to Sugar Mama's?"

"No, but what a great name for an ice cream shop."

"And the ice cream is good too."

"It's settled. I'll accompany you two to ice cream after practice, then follow you home. Another agent will be stationed outside your house overnight."

Her phone pinged to indicate an incoming text. "I've got to check this."

With a smile, she moved away, not at all sure pretending to date Titus was the brightest idea she'd considered—but it certainly was the most tempting.

# CHAPTER 6

"Off to bed with you." Titus closed *The Invention of Hugo Cabret*. He stood to put the children's book on the built-in shelves by the fireplace.

"One more chapter, please?" Sam snuggled under his favorite blanket, the appeal in his brown eyes magnified by his glasses. "I've got to learn more about the mechanical man."

"Sorry, buddy. It's already past your bedtime on a school night."

Sam let out a dramatic sigh and dragged himself from the couch, his blanket balled under his arm. "Okay."

Titus smothered a smile behind his hand as he followed Sam to his son's room down the hall. He didn't blame Sam for wanting more of the illustrated book by Brian Selznick. Titus also wanted to find out how the mechanical man fit into Hugo's story.

After prayers and tucking Sam in, Titus turned off the light and started to close the door.

"Dad?"

Titus poked his head into the room. "Sam, it's late."

"I know. But will you be seeing Ms. Manning again soon? I like her."

"I don't know." Titus paused, then added softly, "I like her too."

In the kitchen, he drummed his fingers on the counter as the empty evening stretched out in front of him like a barren highway. He usually had no problem filling the hours between Sam's bedtime and his own, but tonight, a restlessness consumed him. Chalissa's face filled his mind. This pretending to date might have its privileges—to convince Sam, they'd have to actually go out to dinner a few times. The thought of her sitting across from him at Hamrocks, a candle flickering in the middle of the table as they dined on crab cakes and braised brussels sprouts, brought a smile to his lips. His smile faded as reality horned in on the cozy image. Better not to dwell on what couldn't be. Maybe once he testified...

He shook his head. Nope, the case could drag on for years with appeals. And even if it ended at trial, he would likely still need to stay in WITSEC. Which put the kibosh on having a real relationship with the very pretty inspector. He refused to think about the possibility of going to prison for taking bribes. No way would he contemplate what would happen to Sam in that instance.

Better to steer his attention to figuring out how the video was doctored. The federal prosecutors were looking into that as well, but he'd learned a thing or two about videos during his website design coursework. If he could get a copy of the video, he might be able to find out how they duplicated his voice so precisely. That would have to wait until tomorrow, though.

A cup of decaf coffee might help settle him down. Or at least it would give him something to do. He'd just brewed the cup when his doorbell rang.

Moving to the door, he peered through the peephole. Chalissa Manning stood on the stoop, a tall black man beside her. He opened the door. "Hello, Inspector Manning."

"Good evening, Mr. Davis," the man spoke first. "I'm Deputy Marshal Trevor Chambers." He held out his hand and Titus shook it. "We apologize for showing up unannounced, but may we come in?"

"Of course." Titus stepped back to allow them to enter, then shut the door. "I just made a cup of decaf coffee. Would you like to join me?"

"Yes, that would be lovely." Chalissa shrugged out of her jacket.

"That's a no for me." Chambers shook his head. "My wife's trying to get me to cut back on all kinds of coffee."

"What about a glass of water?" Titus asked.

"Sure," the other man replied.

"I'll be back in a minute. Make yourselves at home." Titus left them to find their own seats in the living room and hurried to make another cup of coffee and pour a glass of filtered water. Remembering how she liked her coffee, he added a small spoonful of sugar and a bit of cream to Chalissa's.

"Here you go." Titus set the cup on a coaster on the low table in front of Chalissa, who had chosen one end of the couch, then handed the glass to Chambers, who sat in the club chair. "Be right back with my coffee."

Titus returned with his cup and settled on the opposite end of the couch. He took a sip before setting his cup on a coaster.

That seemed to be the signal Chambers had been waiting for because he set his own glass down. "Mr. Davis, may we speak freely here?"

"Yes," Titus said. Unease at the Marshal's tone settled hard on his shoulders like a bag of concrete.

"Where is your son?" Chambers asked.

"He's in bed."

"Asleep?" Chambers pressed.

Titus glanced down the hallway toward Sam's closed door. "I'm not sure. We can move downstairs if you're concerned about him overhearing our conversation."

"Perfect." Chambers stood and picked up his water glass, waiting while Chalissa and Titus did the same with their mugs. "Lead the way."

Titus moved to the stairs off the kitchen, then down into what he and Sam used as their TV and game room. Behind him, the two Marshals followed.

Chambers pointed to the two loveseats and recliner, all facing the flat screen TV hanging on the opposite wall. "Mind if I move the recliner?"

"Not at all." Titus assisted the other man in rearranging one loveseat and the recliner into a grouping more conducive to talking. He dropped down beside Chalissa on the loveseat while her boss took the recliner. Breathing in, he caught a whiff of a floral scent on Chalissa. Maybe lavender? Subtly taking another deep breath, he zeroed in on the scent. Definitely lavender. His mother had dried herbs and he'd loved helping her as a child. Lavender had been one of his favorite scents. He'd given Eve a bottle of lavender oil for her birthday when they were dating but she'd hardly worn what she labeled as a "commonplace" scent, preferring expensive manufactured perfumes.

Chambers sipped his water, then put the glass on the floor beside his seat.

Titus brought his own cup to his lips and drank, hoping the hot liquid would divert his thoughts from the pleasant-smelling woman beside him.

"Inspector Manning brought your pretend dating suggestion to me for approval," Chambers began. "The Marshal Service has a strict policy of no fraternizing between witnesses and inspectors. The #MeToo movement aside, we've always strived to enforce our procedures."

Titus nodded, then added when the other man didn't immediately continue, "I understand."

"Good. Inspector Manning said your main concern was preserving your identity in WITSEC from your son. As a father myself, I understand your desire to keep Sam safe."

Titus looked from Chalissa to Chambers. "Earlier tonight, when she told me about the threat sent to the courthouse, all I could think of was not frightening Sam by having strangers hanging around us. He's on this kick to find me a date. Not sure why, but who knows how a seven-year-old's brain works? So it seemed like us pretending to go out might make things easier on Sam." Titus rubbed the back of his suddenly hot neck. "But the more I thought about it, the more I realized it wasn't a smart move. I'm sorry, Inspector Manning."

"It's okay." She cleared her throat. "It's actually not a bad idea. We don't want to draw unwanted attention to you, but we do need to step up security. Having us seem like we're together would make things much simpler to anyone watching you as well."

"The upside," Chambers interjected, "would be that Sam wouldn't be in jeopardy of accidentally figuring out what's really going on. I think it could work. Inspector Manning has been briefed on how to handle the more, well, intimate appearance of your interactions." Chambers stood. "I'll let her fill you in on the details."

Titus started to rise, but Chambers waved him back down. "Inspector Manning can show me out."

Chalissa followed Chambers up the stairs. Titus moved the recliner back to its original position. He'd just retaken his seat when she returned to join him on the loveseat.

Chalissa met his eyes, a faint blush washing over her pale cheeks. "Apparently, it wasn't such a bad idea after all."

He let his gaze linger a moment on her face, the attention deepening the blush. That gave him courage to say what he had been thinking when Chambers approved the plan to keep Sam unaware of WITSEC. "Is it okay to say I'm glad of the chance to get to know you better, even under such awkward circumstances?"

His question brought a slight curl to the corners of her lips, although she didn't allow the smile to grow. "I think so too." Breaking eye contact, she withdrew a folded piece of paper from her bag. "We need to go over the ground rules, then we both have to sign this consent form. First, no overnight stays, even in separate rooms."

"I wholeheartedly agree." Titus matched her solemn tone.

"For physical touches, and to make this believable to anyone observing us, we can hold hands."

"Like this?" He reached over and gently took her hand in his, intertwining their fingers.

The blush returned to her cheeks. "That's acceptable." She extracted her hand and clasped hers together. "A hand on and around shoulders, short hugs, that sort of thing is okay too."

"Got it. Think 1950s public displays of affection."

She shot him a grateful smile. "Exactly."

He shared the smile, then dropped his gaze to her mouth. "What about kissing?" Titus hadn't meant to ask that question, but since he had been looking at her lips, it had popped out.

A strand of dark auburn hair brushed her face, and he gave into the impulse to tuck it behind her ear. The air hummed around them as if suspended by a forklift.

"Dad!" Sam's terrified cry rang out from upstairs. "Help!"

# CHAPTER 7

C halissa leapt to her feet to dash after Titus, who had run for the stairs at his son's cry. At the top of the stairs, she drew her gun before hitting the light switch to flood the darkened living room. Nothing.

She peered up the short flight of stairs leading to the bedrooms of the split-level home. Light spilled out of an open doorway. Sam's shuddering sobs and Titus's murmurings indicated no one else's presence in the boy's room.

After checking the locks on the front door, she systematically checked every window on the main floor, then the two bedrooms and bathrooms on the upper level. She returned downstairs to do the same, ending her sweep of the house at the French doors leading to the patio. Nothing unlocked. A wall clock read eight thirty. The overnight security team would be in place at nine, her estimated time of departure. A check outside was warranted, but first she'd hear what triggered the scream.

Holstering her weapon, she headed back upstairs. Titus stood by the stove, stirring something in a pan over a lit burner.

"How's Sam?" She peered into the pan. Milk gently swirled around as he moved a wooden spoon in a circle.

"Scared." Titus turned off the burner and poured the warm milk into a waiting mug. "I've never seen him this upset."

"Nightmare?"

He shook his head and picked up the mug. "He says no."

"Then what happened? I did a thorough check of the house. Everything's secure with no sign of disturbance on any of the windows or doors."

"I think you need to hear it for yourself. Come on. He's calmed down enough to talk with you."

She followed Titus to Sam's room, waiting in the doorway while he carried the cup to where Sam lay huddled under the blankets on a twin bed. "Hey, buddy. I brought you some warm milk."

"Okay." Sam pushed himself to a sitting position and accepted the mug from his dad.

Chalissa leaned against the door frame, watching as Titus adjusted the covers around Sam's legs while the boy took a sip from the mug.

"Do you think you can tell Ms. Manning what happened?" Titus smoothed back hair that had flopped onto Sam's forehead.

"I guess so." Sam raised the mug for another sip.

Titus beckoned Chalissa to approach the bed.

She moved to the opposite side from Titus and sat near the foot. Sam looked at her with wary eyes, tension radiating like steam from his little frame. Best not to be too direct in her questioning, or she wouldn't get much from him before he dissolved into tears again. "What did you do after dinner tonight?"

Sam wrinkled his nose. "Not much because I had to finish a math worksheet. Dad read to me before bed."

"What book?" Chalissa cocked her head slightly to one side, never averting her gaze from Sam's face.

His eyes brightened behind his glasses. "*The Invention of Hugo Cabret.*"

At the enthusiasm in his voice, she smiled. "Ah, a favorite of yours, I think."

Sam bobbed his head up and down. "Yes. It's about a boy who lives in a train station and he meets a girl, then an old man. Lots of stuff happens." He glanced at Titus. "Dad stopped at the really good part about the mechanical man, but it's a school night, so…." He shrugged without finishing his thought.

"Bummer, but you'll be able to hear more of the story tomorrow night," she said.

"Maybe you'll read it to me?" The eagerness in his voice touched her heart, but she had to douse his expectation. She didn't want to hurt Sam by becoming too involved in his life while pretending to date his father.

"Ms. Manning's job keeps her awfully busy," Titus cut in.

Seeing Sam's lower lip start to jut out, she interjected, "But not too busy that I can't stop by for a chapter or two. Hugo sounds like a very interesting boy."

"He is," Sam said. "Do you want to know what's happened in the book so far?"

"Sure." Chalissa settled her back against the wall and listened as Sam recounted, in a convoluted sort of way, the story of Hugo. The more he talked, the more relaxed his demeanor became. Good, he'd be more likely to recall what happened to make him scream now that his body wasn't in the fight, flight, or freeze mode.

"And that's what Hugo did in the chapter Dad read tonight." Sam sipped his milk.

"Thank you. I'm looking forward to reading about Hugo's adventures soon." She softened her voice even more. "Can you tell me why you woke up?"

Sam frowned, and the mug of milk tipped toward the bedspread. Titus rescued it before any liquid spilled.

"The song."

She leaned closer, not sure she heard the quiet response. Titus started to say something, but she laid a hand on his arm to stop him. Better to let Sam tell the story in his own way. But when Sam didn't continue, she prompted, "Was it music or words?"

"Music," Sam responded quickly.

47

"Could you identify the instrument?" Chalissa asked.

"Guitar." Sam turned to his father. "It sounded like the one Pastor Warren plays during the song service at church."

"An acoustic guitar," Titus clarified for Chalissa.

"Was it a tune you recognized?" she said.

"Not at first," Sam said. "Then it sounded like 'Twinkle, Twinkle Little Star.'"

Titus sucked in a breath but didn't say anything. She made a mental note to ask him about the song's significance later. "Where was the music coming from?"

The boy scrunched up his face. "It sounded far away, then got louder."

"Inside the room or outside?" she prompted.

"Not inside," Sam said.

"Outside the window perhaps?" Chalissa rose to examine the room's single window on the wall perpendicular to the boy's bed.

"Maybe."

Stars dotted the pale blue curtains, which had been pushed opened. She felt along the top of the window to the latch. Tightly closed and locked. "Were the curtains closed or open when you went to bed?"

Sam looked down at the bedspread. "Closed, but I wanted to look at the sky, so I opened them." He turned to his father. "Sorry I got out of bed."

Titus hugged his son. "It's okay. I know how much you like to see the stars at night."

"But if I hadn't pushed the curtains open, I wouldn't have seen the face."

"A face?" Chalissa turned from her examination of the window. Sam shivered.

Titus set the mug on the dresser next to the bed, then gathered his son into his arms. From the safety of his father's embrace, Sam said, "Yeah, outside the window."

Again, Titus opened his mouth, but Chalissa caught his eye and shook her head to keep him silent. To her relief, he obeyed her unspoken signal. She was building a rapport with Sam she didn't want broken. She suspected Sam had told her more than he'd revealed to his father, which was understandable since Sam was calmer now.

"What did you notice about the face?" Reaching into the back pocket of her jeans, she pulled her phone out and swiped it open. Quickly opening a recording app, she started recording so she didn't miss Sam's description. Openly taking notes might spook him more.

"He had on a Washington Nationals baseball cap."

The detail surprised her. "Did he?"

"I recognized the curly W," Sam replied. "Dad took me to a game last summer. I have a baseball hat just like the man's."

"It was a man who peered in your window?"

Sam nodded.

She took in his serious face and hated that she had to press him. "How could you tell if you weren't wearing your glasses?"

"But I was." Sam squirmed in his father's arms. "I wanted to see if I could find the Big Dipper from my bed, so I was wearing my glasses." He hung his head. "Sorry, Dad. I know I'm not supposed to put them on when the lights are out."

"It's okay." Titus brushed a kiss on Sam's forehead.

She asked the next logical question, "Did you recognize the face?"

"No," Sam whispered. "But he knew me."

Chalissa stifled a gasp. "How do you know?"

Sam snuggled closer to his father. "He called me Sam."

Titus looked down at Sam. "How did you hear the man through the closed window?"

"He said my name."

Titus tried to keep his voice level as anger rose inside him like hot asphalt bubbling in the mixer. "Are you sure?"

Sam's voice had a timid edge to it. "I saw his lips form my name."

His son trembled in his arms. They needed to tread lightly or Sam would clam up and not answer any more questions.

Chalissa touched Titus's arm. "I think we can let Sam go back to sleep now." She smiled at Sam. "You've been very helpful, but you've had enough excitement for now. We can talk about it again in the morning."

"Okay." Sam smothered a yawn and his eyelids drooped. Titus removed Sam's glasses, then tucked the covers around his son's shoulders. Out of the corner of his eye, he spied Chalissa pulling the curtains closed before leaving the room. He prayed for Sam to have sweet and undisturbed dreams, then carried the almost-empty mug of milk into the kitchen. Chalissa leaned against a counter, her attention on her phone. He rinsed out the mug and put it in the dishwasher, then washed the pan.

"Thanks for not pushing Sam for more details." Titus paused, searching for how to express his gratitude for her reading of the situation. Sam did not react well under pressure, especially when he was scared. Most kids probably didn't, but Sam wasn't like most kids.

"Better he go to sleep than keep him up going over it again and again. He'll likely remember more in the morning, if there's more to recall," she said. "I called Chambers. A team will be out tomorrow morning to investigate the yard and area under Sam's window."

"Eve used to sing that song to Sam when he was fussy as a baby. He loved that song." Titus scrubbed a hand over his face.

"It's also a very popular children's nursery rhyme. I know this scared you and Sam."

"You bet it did." Even now, fear nipped at his heels like a junkyard dog. "It must mean someone has discovered I'm hiding in WITSEC." His voice shook as his initial anger gave way to relief that Sam was safe. He drew in a breath to steady his nerves. "Are we even safe in our home?"

"For now, I think you are." Her calm voice soothed him. "Sam was sleepy. There's a chance he saw a reflection in the glass and imagined someone was there."

"He was so certain." Sam always told the truth. But a part of him wondered if maybe his son had picked up on his own anxiety about the video and had "seen" something as a result.

"Kids like Sam—"

"What's that supposed to mean?" Every time he turned around, he ran into someone only seeing Sam's diagnosis and not the boy for the wonderful individual he was.

"That sometimes, kids with autism don't always see things the way other kids do."

The truth didn't stop him from lashing out. "What does a single woman without kids know about raising a child on the autism spectrum?"

To his horror, he caught a glimpse of tears in Chalissa's eyes before she whipped her body around, avoiding his gaze.

He opened his mouth to apologize for being insensitive, when she turned back, her eyes bright but clear. "Don't worry, *Mr. Davis,* we won't assume Sam is making up what he saw. We will step up security as we discussed, but the best thing for you and Sam is to carry on as usual."

"Chalissa, I'm sor—"

Her phone pinged, cutting off his apology. "The overnight detail has arrived. That's my cue to leave." She headed for the door.

Titus hurried after her. "Wait."

Her hand reached for the doorknob.

"Please." To his relief, she didn't open the door.

"I'm sorry. Will you forgive me? I shouldn't have allowed my protectiveness of Sam to cause me to lose my manners." For a heart-beat, he thought she would simply walk out the door.

"It's okay. It's been a stressful night." Then she slipped out the door and into the cool spring evening. Titus shoved the deadbolt home with a snick and a heavy heart. Somehow, his careless remark had hurt Chalissa, and it would take more than an apology to put it right. Perhaps flowers would smooth things over. He'd choose something extra special to send to her office.

51

# CHAPTER 8

"Is there anything to support Sam's story?" Chalissa twirled a pencil around her fingers as she listened to the verbal report on the phone from Brian Smithers, who headed the Marshal's technology and evidence department. A team had just returned to the lab after examining the scene.

"Yes and no," Brian said.

"I'm all ears." She tapped the notepad with the pencil and waited.

"No discernible footprints near the window."

"I figured there wouldn't be—it's been dry lately."

"But we did luck out with a partial fingerprint on the window frame."

"Any hits?" She doodled a window frame.

"Nope, but all that means is he's not in the system," Brian replied.

"What about the neighbors?"

"No one saw anything at most of the homes. We still have one more home to check out. No one answered the door at the house to the left."

"That's the one closest to Sam's window?" She added a flower box to her window, shading in the drawing to give a more three-dimensional shape.

"Right, so we'll head back out there around dinnertime to see if we can check with them. If we're lucky, they'll have noticed something."

"Okay, thanks for the update." She ended the call, then tossed the pencil down. Had Titus's WITSEC identity been blown? Apparently, Sam hadn't been imagining things outside his window last night. She pulled up the form to request the Davises be moved to a safe house as a precaution until they could determine whether or not Titus's identity had been compromised.

TITUS KEYED IN THE TEXT TO CREATE A POPUP BOX FOR A CLIENT'S doggy daycare and boarding website. Pampered Paws had been one of the first websites he'd designed for Spider Web Design, and the owner had requested Titus be on the account permanently. More than a few of his design clients had signed on to Spider Web Design's ongoing maintenance agreement, with Titus as their designated employee.

"Did you hear?"

He hit save, then swiveled to see Terrick Moreston standing by his cubicle. "Probably not. I've not made it to the break room yet today." Which meant he hadn't heard any office gossip.

Since Monday's merger meeting, rumors had been flying about pending layoffs and reorganization within the company. Everyone had a theory about who would be let go and why, but as of Wednesday morning, nothing had happened.

"Dwayne was let go an hour ago."

Titus gaped at Terrick. "Seriously?"

Terrick nodded and leaned closer. "Molly Carstairs was walking by Ned Turner's office when it happened. She said Dwayne and Ned were shouting at each other behind closed doors."

"Oh, man." The conversation Titus had with Dwayne flashed into his mind. The man had projected anger and hurt mingled together as he'd talked about his early days with Spider Web Design. "Hey, did you know Dwayne started the company with Jamie Hewson?"

Terrick snorted. "No way. Must be Dwayne's vivid imagination."

Titus wasn't so sure, but he only had his gut feeling to back it up. "He has been at the company a long time. Being downsized has got to hurt."

"Yeah, but he was fired, not let go."

"Same difference—he's out of a job."

"It's not the same. Molly overheard Dwayne protesting he was being fired so he couldn't cash in on the merger," Terrick said. "If you're fired, you don't get severance or any stock options, etc."

"How do you know all this?"

"It's in the contract we all signed," he shrugged. "I reviewed it earlier this week because of the merger. Wanted to know my rights."

"Makes sense." A ping alerted Titus to an incoming text. "I'd better get this."

"See you later," Terrick said as he left.

Titus checked the text on his personal phone. It was from a number he didn't recognize.

*Get out of the building now.*

CHALISSA HEADED ACROSS THE PARKING LOT TOWARD THE BUILDING where Titus worked, the aroma of Chinese food wafting from the bag she carried. The bouquet of spring flowers Titus had sent to her office, along with the heartfelt apology penned on the card, had erased the hurt of his words the night before. Titus had no way of knowing just how much experience Chalissa had with autism. She'd wrestled half the night with her own overly-sensitive reaction, so the flowers had given her a chance to accept his apology more fully. At least the flowers provided more "evidence" for their dating cover.

She'd reached out by email to see about taking him to lunch, but Titus said his Wednesday schedule wouldn't accommodate leaving work to eat. In the lobby, she stopped to confer with the inspector on duty, who sat reading a newspaper in a small grouping of chairs. A quick glance revealed no one close enough to overhear their conversation. "Hey, Eli. How's it going?"

Eli Farrell folded his newspaper and rose from a club chair. "Quiet. Nothing out of the ordinary that I can tell. The building security has been cooperative about double checking unknown delivery personnel and visitors."

A middle-aged woman in a beige uniform with her hair scraped back into a tight bun manned the desk near the elevators in the spacious lobby. The guard sat glued to her phone, long red lacquered nails swiping up and down on the screen. "She seems absorbed in her work."

He laughed. "Stacy's okay. She spent four years as a beat cop before an on-the-job injury made standing for long periods of time difficult. She's been here ever since."

"I shouldn't let appearances deceive me?"

"Exactly. Nothing gets by Stacy."

"Good to know. When will your relief come?"

Eli pulled out his phone and tapped the screen. "In half an hour. Are you leaving the building?"

She held up the bag of food. "No, we'll eat lunch in one of the conference rooms."

Eli walked her over to the elevator banks and pressed the up button. "He's on the ninth floor."

"Thanks." The elevator doors opened and she entered, punching the ninth floor button. A soft ping alerted her to a text. Juggling the food bag, she managed to access her phone. Three text messages from Titus.

The first message was time-stamped fifteen minutes ago, when she had been in the car and had her phone on Do Not Disturb While Driving.

*I know you're on your way, but got this strange message: Get out of the building now.*

The second message came three minutes later.

*Should I go to the lobby?*

The third message came on top of one another.

*Something's not right.*

Chalissa set the bag on the floor and checked her Glock. Loaded and ready. For now, she left it in her waist holster. The elevator smoothly arrived at the ninth floor. When the doors opened, Chalissa stepped out, her senses on high alert to potential danger. No more texts from Titus, though she'd tried to reach him by phone and text during the ride up.

No one sat behind the glass reception desk. She put the takeout on the desk and pulled out her phone to text Eli.

*Can't reach Titus. Call for backup. Got a bad feeling.*

Turning her phone to vibrate, she slipped it into her pocket. With her hand on the butt of her Glock, she cautiously eased toward the closed door leading back to the offices. Encountering a locked handle, Chalissa texted Eli again, asking him to get the security guard to remotely unlock the door. His affirmative response came back immediately, along with the ETA of backup from the local police and Marshal field office. With what had happened outside Sam's window the night before, they were taking no chances to keep Titus and Sam safe.

*Is someone going to Sam's school?* Chalissa texted Eli.

Eli replied: *Yes, Mac will check in at the school to make sure he's safe. Try the door now, should be open.*

Chalissa checked the handle, finding it moved easily. She slowly opened the door. She tried to remember what she'd learned about the layout of Spider Web Design's offices. A circle, with Titus's cubicle toward the south when you exited the elevators. Which meant she should turn right.

Silence greeted her, along with signs of hasty departures on the desks of the cubicles she passed. Lunch wrappings on the floor, folders spilled haphazardly on a desk, a few chairs tipped on their sides.

Systematically, she cleared each work space on the right, then peeked into the opposite office lining the outer ring of the workspace. Four offices down, a closed door made her heart skip a beat. She checked behind her, then put her hand on the knob and twisted. Locked.

A muffled sob drew her attention. Someone was inside.

# CHAPTER 9

Chalissa dropped into a crouched position outside the office. She put her mouth near the door seam and spoke softly. "I'm a U.S. Marshal. Are you okay?"

For several seconds, no one responded. Maybe she'd imagined the sound. Then the door slowly opened enough for Chalissa to slip inside. She did so quickly, closing the door without a sound behind her. The drawn shades on both the outer window and the inner one made the room dim, but she spotted two women huddled together near a desk. Academy training cautioned against moving too deeply into the office until she knew what was going on. "Why are you hiding?"

"Dwayne Redman came in yelling he had a bomb," the younger woman said, her body shaking despite her arms wrapped tightly around her raised knees. "He demanded everyone go to the conference room."

An older woman laid her hand on her coworker's shoulder.

"What are your names?" Chalissa maintained a calm tone despite the circumstances.

"I'm Doris," the older of the two women responded. "This is Yvette."

"I'm Chalissa. Now who's Dwayne?"

"He's worked here for years," piped a voice from behind the desk.

Chalissa moved around the desk to see a third woman had her back against the wall with the head of a middle-aged man on her lap. "I'm Jill, and this is Terrick."

Doris pushed hair off her forehead with a trembling hand. "I think Terrick had a heart attack."

Chalissa holstered her weapon as she evaluated the man with a visual sweep across his body, noting his pale face. She longed to pepper the women with more questions, but clearly the man needed assistance. "What were his symptoms?"

Jill's eyes welled. "In the hallway, he clutched his arm, then collapsed. We managed to get him into this office and lock the door."

The man's pasty complexion worried Chalissa. She placed her fingers on his neck for a pulse. "His heartbeat is faint but steady. How long ago did this happen?"

"Maybe ten minutes," Doris said.

"I've already called for backup, so EMTs and police should be here any minute. We'll get him out of here as soon as we can do so safely. In the meantime, we should keep him warm. Anyone have a jacket to drape over him?"

"I think Mr. Turner—it's his office we're in—keeps a sports coat in his office." Jill pointed to a sleeve dangling from a hook on the back of the door.

Doris tugged the garment from its hanger and passed it to Chalissa, who tucked the tweed sports coat around Terrick. "Did you check his pockets for aspirin or nitroglycerin tabs? If he has a bad heart, he might keep those on him."

The women shook their heads, so Chalissa rummaged through Terrick's pants pockets. Nothing. She tried the front shirt pocket and found a small packet of pills. Squinting in the low light, she made out the name Bayer Aspirin. She tore open the packet and emptied the two uncoated tablets into her hand. Shaking his shoulder, she said, "Terrick, can you hear me?"

No movement. She tried again, a little louder. This time, he opened his eyes. "We think you had a heart attack. I need you to chew these tablets."

He nodded and Chalissa placed the medication in his open mouth. "Help is on the way." With first aid administered, she could question the women. "What happened?"

"Mr. Turner fired Dwayne this morning. Because of the merger," Jill said.

"With a marketing company, right?" Titus had mentioned something about a merger over ice cream the night before.

"Yes," Doris said. "Mr. Turner's let go several others today."

"Did any of you actually see Dwayne with a bomb?" Chalissa needed to know if the device was on his person or if he might have hidden it somewhere on the floor.

"I'm not sure, but I did see Dwayne," Yvette said.

"Can you describe what he was wearing?" Chalissa straightened.

"A long-sleeved flannel shirt, jeans, and some sort of hunter's or fishing vest."

Chalissa leaned toward Yvette. "Did the vest bulge or lay flat against his chest?"

Yvette scrunched up her nose as if concentrating on remembering. "It appeared bulky."

Not good. That meant the vest likely concealed or contained the bomb. "Where did Dwayne go?"

"He shouted for everyone to get to Conference Room A," Jill said. "I heard the commotion from the lavatory next to the break room. Doris managed to get away and warned me. We waited until the coast was clear before leaving. That's when Yvette beckoned us into this office, saying Terrick wasn't doing well."

Chalissa patted his arm, then turned back to the women. "Now tell me where the conference room is."

"It's to the left when you leave this office, about halfway around from the lobby door you entered," Doris said.

Chalissa thought about how far she'd come already. "So not too far from this office?"

"It's about six offices down," the older woman replied.

"Give me the layout of the room." Chalissa needed specifics. She opened another text to Eli as Doris explained.

Chalissa texted Eli the updated information, including details on where she thought Dwayne had the bomb.

"It has windows on the outside with blinds, and windows on the inside with blinds too. Two doors on either end," Doris said. "Inside, there's a large table that seats twenty, with chairs along the walls between the doors and by the windows for another twenty."

"How many people could be inside the room?" Chalissa texted the info to Eli.

Doris exchanged a look with Jill, then Yvette. Jill said, "There's about a hundred people working here, but I don't know how many have been laid off because of the merger."

"An estimate as to how many people are still here?" Chalissa stood and flexed her shoulders to work out any kinks before leaving the room.

"Possibly around forty people," Doris estimated.

After sending that data to Eli, Chalissa pulled out her gun and chambered a bullet before moving to the door.

"You're leaving us?" Yvette's voice held a note of panic.

"You'll be safe here. I let my colleague know where you are and that you need medical assistance." Chalissa put her hand on the door-knob. "No matter what you hear, don't open the door until police or EMTs arrive."

The women nodded. Drawing in a deep breath, Chalissa left the sanctuary of the office and headed down the hallway to the conference room.

"Everyone in the conference room, or I blow this place up right now!" Dwayne clutched an object in his left hand.

Titus followed his coworkers into the largest of the two conference rooms. After years of living a quiet life, he had forgotten how pulse-pounding fear invaded one's entire body. A picture of Sam flashed across his mind. He would not make Sam an orphan. Not on his watch. He'd do whatever it took to get back to his son alive.

"Get these chairs out of here." Dwayne paced near the door, his eyes magnified behind his glasses. "And close the blinds."

Titus helped move the rolling conference chairs into the hallway. A few people hurried over to the windows and yanked down the blinds as Dwayne hit the light switch.

"Everyone on the floor." Sweat blanketed Dwayne's forehead despite the cool office temperature. "No talking!"

Titus scrambled with everyone else to find a seat while Dwayne muttered under his breath words Titus couldn't decipher. No one spoke, the silence punctuated by muffled sobs from some of the women.

"Listen, Dwayne," Jamie Hewson said from across the room.

"I said no talking." Dwayne leveled his gaze at the CEO.

Titus sat with his back against the outer wall, his legs outstretched. He hoped Chalissa received his texts. Surely help must be on the way. The young woman beside him, a recent hire in the sales department, snuffled into a tissue. The sound must have reached Dwayne's ears because he swiveled his body toward them. When his gaze fell on Titus, anger darkened Dwayne's features.

Jabbing his finger at Titus, Dwayne growled, "I told you to get out of here."

Titus had figured out too late the cryptic text had been sent by Dwayne. "I know." Despite his pounding heart, Titus managed to keep his voice conversational.

"Then why are you still here?" Dwayne asked.

"I was heading out when I got pulled into a meeting," Titus said, hoping it sounded like the truth.

"No, no, no, no!" His reply seemed to make Dwayne even more agitated. The man resumed pacing, his lips moving but no sound emitted.

"What do you want?" Porter Lansing piped up from across the room, his tone combative.

Just what the situation didn't need, but Porter was too far away for Titus to warn him not to mess with Dwayne.

Dwayne stopped close to Titus, his attention fixed on Porter. "I want you to be quiet!"

Dwayne's proximity afforded Titus a closer view of his vest and his heart sank. The garment bulged in the chest area. Even to his untrained eyes, it appeared Dwayne hadn't been lying about carrying a bomb. Maybe if he distracted Dwayne, he could buy enough time for help to arrive. *Please God, don't let anyone get hurt.*

"Dwayne," Titus began. "You have our attention. Why don't you tell us why you're doing this?"

His coworker blinked, then slowly nodded. "Because he stole it." Dwayne swung around to point at Jamie, who mopped the moisture from his forehead with a snowy white handkerchief. "Tell them how you stole my ideas to start this company, then sold me out."

Jamie replaced the handkerchief in his back pocket. "I didn't steal your ideas."

"Not the right answer." Dwayne waved his arm. "*I* created the websites. *You* took all the credit. That's stealing."

Titus eased his phone out and snapped a picture of Dwayne while the man argued with the company president.

"You were paid, quite handsomely I might add." Jamie sounded peeved, not how Titus would have responded to a maniac with a bomb strapped to his chest.

"It was never about the money!" Dwayne slammed his fist against the conference table. "We were partners, but you pushed me to the fringes because you wanted more. I should have realized how greedy you were becoming. This merger proved it. You fired me to avoid paying me my share of profits from the merger."

"Now, that's not true." Jamie's tone rang false to Titus's ears. "You were terminated because your job performance has not been up to par lately."

Dwayne snorted. "And yet at my last review six months ago, my coworkers and clients had nothing but positive things to say about my work."

"That was true, but it's your, uh, *personality* that can be rather abrasive," Jamie retorted. "And this stunt proves we were right to be concerned."

Someone's cell phone trilled, making several people, including Titus, jump.

"Shut that off!" Dwayne yelled, his head swiveling around the room to find the source of the sound. The guilty party, a young man in website design, scrambled to silence the device, but he had no sooner stopped the sound than another phone went off, followed by another. Soon the entire room filled with the sound of pinging and ringing phones.

Titus checked his own device, his heart beating faster at a text from Chalissa: *The police sent texts and calls to all employee cell numbers they could find. Anything I should know? I'm right outside the door.*

He quickly replied: *Dwayne Redman with bomb vest. Here's a pic.*

Dwayne swung his head back and forth. "Turn off your phones! Now!"

Turning his phone to silent mode, he lowered the volume as well. In the sudden silence, Dwayne pressed his hands against the sides of his head. The man seemed to be hanging on by a quickly unraveling thread.

Then the landline conference table phone rang, the sound shrill in the quiet room.

"Answer it!" Dwayne directed his command at a senior administrative assistant, who crawled over and pressed the speaker button on the conference phone in the middle of the table.

"Dwayne Redman, this is Captain Stone, with the Fairfax County Police Department."

# CHAPTER 10

As Captain Stone tried to open negotiations with Dwayne, Titus used the table's edge to cover his movement and slipped his phone from his pocket.

The more the captain talked, the more relaxed Dwayne's body language became. The man nearly smiled at one point, nodding his head as Stone continued to ask questions designed to lower Dwayne's guard. Little did the woman know it had the opposite effect, as Dwayne instead regained his composure and confidence.

Titus thumbed a text to Chalissa: *Don't believe any concessions. Dwayne not going to cooperate.*

Her reply came back swiftly: *Out of my hands. Still in hallway. With explosive vest, not going to chance direct assault until other avenues fully explored.*

He slowly eased down until he was sitting nearly underneath the table. Dwayne and the captain continued to talk, but the placid tone to his coworker's voice told Titus time was running out. Dwayne had already decided on a course of action. Now that the negotiator had called, everything was back on track.

Titus sent another text to Chalissa: *Not much time. Dwayne's lying.*

*Plan B it is. Does Dwayne have a hand-held trigger?*

*Yes, in left hand.*

*Is his finger on a trigger or do you think the bomb isn't armed yet?*

*Will check.*

He put the phone into his back pocket and craned his neck to see Dwayne's legs moving back and forth on the long side of the table.

"I want a helicopter and three million dollars," Dwayne said.

"That'll take some time," the captain replied, her voice as smooth as freshly leveled cement. "In the meantime, how about a goodwill gesture?"

"Like releasing one of my hostages?"

"That would be a good start," Captain Stone said.

Titus scooted to the left to get a view of Dwayne. He held the trigger device loosely, no fingers pressing down on the top or clutching the side. Must not be armed then.

"Sure, I can do that." Dwayne punched off the call.

Fear wrapped an icy hand around Titus's heart and squeezed. Something about Dwayne's almost jovial tone made him think time wasn't on his side. He reached for his phone to text Chalissa.

"Titus?" Dwayne's question halted his movement.

Reluctantly, he left the phone in his back pocket and stood. His coworkers lined up against the wall of floor-to-ceiling windows avoided his gaze.

Drawing in a deep breath, Titus faced Dwayne across the polished surface of the conference table. His colleague nodded once. The landline rang again. Titus winced.

Dwayne hit the speaker button. "Captain, I have the name of the hostage I'll release."

"Good, I'll make arrangements—"

"Titus Davis will be walking out the door in five seconds." Dwayne ended the call. He had spoken over the negotiator's words as if the woman hadn't talked at all. His eyes on Titus, Dwayne said, "You should have left when I sent you that text."

"Don't do this, Dwayne." Titus looked at the other hostages, then back to Dwayne. "Send one of the women instead."

Shaking his head, Dwayne pointed his finger at the door. "It's time for you to leave."

"Let's talk about this for a minute," Titus said.

"Leave." Dwayne expression didn't waver.

Titus moved slowly past his colleagues toward the door on the right, farthest away from where Dwayne paced. He reached the door just as Dwayne uttered, "The clock is ticking. You have two seconds left."

Without looking back, Titus tugged open the door. Someone dressed in full SWAT team gear yanked him into the hallway as the door slammed shut behind him.

CHALISSA PLACED A STEAMING CUP OF COFFEE INTO TITUS'S HANDS. Her witness sat on the curb at the back of the parking lot, a blanket draped around his shoulders. "Drink it," she commanded when he made no move to sip the liquid.

He glanced down at the cup but made no move to obey. "He's going to blow up the room and kill everyone."

"You don't know that. The negotiator and the response team are good at their jobs." She sat beside him, close enough that their shoulders touched. Chalissa glanced back toward the building. Emergency vehicles blocked access, while SWAT teams, cops, and firefighters milled around in organized chaos.

"He texted me to leave." Titus sighed, a long release of air.

"I know." The guilt over so few words tugged at her heart, but she couldn't indulge in the comfort she wanted to give. Instead, she nudged his arm gently to avoid spilling his coffee. "Now drink. You need something hot inside you to counteract the shock."

He shook his head. "I—"

She switched tactics, making her voice businesslike. "You won't be any help to anyone if you're passed out from delayed shock. They might have more questions for you as things progress, so drink the coffee."

He grimaced, but to her relief, raised the cup and sipped. "What did you put in this?"

"Lots of sugar," she smiled at his lip curl. "To counter the shock."

"You keep saying I'm in shock. But I feel fine. In fact, I want to do more to help than sit here away from all the action." He began to rise, but she placed a hand on his arm.

"Stay put." She leaned closer even though no one was within hearing distance. "My number-one priority is to keep you safe. Until we know all the facts, we can't risk you being involved any more than you already are."

"You think this could be tied to my testimony?" He drank more of his coffee, his body appearing to relax slightly as the sugar hit his system.

"We can't rule out the possibility." The FBI was investigating if Dwayne's actions were tied to Titus, but she would keep that tidbit to herself. Witnesses couldn't be privy to everything going on behind the scenes. Usually she didn't mind the secrets, but with Titus, it felt wrong to not tell him everything. Giving herself a firm mental shake, she focused on the man beside her.

"I don't believe it." He gazed at the building. "Someone put Dwayne up to it?"

"I know it sounds crazy, but the timing makes it suspicious."

"Why warn me?"

"You tell me."

"I don't know." He downed the rest of his coffee, his heartbeat slowing down, along with his thought process. "Maybe because I actually listened when Dwayne talked."

"Dwayne wasn't popular with your colleagues?"

"No. He could be annoying."

"In what way?"

"He would fixate on one topic for days on end." He smiled. "A few years ago, he'd buttonhole anyone to talk about the Christmas village he was building in his basement. He invited Sam and me over to see the finished product. It was amazing. Dwayne had hand-carved all the town buildings. Sam loved the working train that surrounded the village. It reminded me of those old-fashioned Currier & Ives holiday paintings."

From Titus's description, Chalissa could picture the village. "You liked him."

"Yeah. Most people went out of their way to avoid him. I think he was lonely." He set his cup in the gutter near his feet.

"What made you see him differently?"

"He reminded me of Sam."

The simplicity of his answer caught her off guard, reminding her sharply of why she tried to be kind to strangers who reminded her of Brandon. "That's," she cleared her throat, "very kind of you."

Titus shrugged, the movement sending the blanket to the sidewalk. Without thinking, she reached around him to re-secure the covering, tucking it closer to him. A breeze wafted over them, rustling the newly budded trees and sending a shaft of cold down Chalissa's spine.

"You're chilly." He leaned away from her slightly to disengage the blanket from under his left leg. Holding out his left arm behind her, he simply said, "Come here."

Her mind screamed this was a bad idea, but another shiver raced through her body, pushing her toward the warmth he was offering. She swayed ever so slightly toward him. He wrapped his arm—and blanket—around her shoulders. The gesture brought her right shoulder and leg into contact with his as the blanket settled around them both. Her head drifted down to his shoulder as if guided there by an unseen hand. This was unprofessional. She should remove herself immediately. But she'd never felt so safe, so secure, and she didn't want the feeling to end. For as long as she could remember, she had been the one who had to stay strong, who couldn't seek rest. She'd learned at a young age that Brandon needed her to look out for him, even though he was older. And she'd gladly taken on that responsibility because she'd loved her brother and he had loved her.

"Better?" His whispered breath sent shivers of a different kind throughout her body and she could only nod against his shoulder.

The melee near the building faded into the distance as the breeze kicked up, a cold undertone despite the late April date. Titus tightened his arm around her, drawing her even closer to him. With a soft sigh, Chalissa closed her eyes, giving herself permission to enjoy the moment.

"Chalissa?"

She opened her eyes, sitting up so fast she nearly clocked his chin with the top of her head. "What?" Had she fallen asleep? Surely not. No way she'd take a nap in the middle of a crisis.

"Your phone's going off," Titus pointed to her pocket where the muffled ring continued.

"Oh, thanks." Using his shoulder as leverage as she stood, she extracted the phone and clicked on. "Chalissa Manning."

"Mac here. How's Davis?"

Chalissa glanced down at Titus, who had tugged the blanket back around his shoulders. He'd closed his eyes, but his lips moved. Was he praying?

"You still there?" Mac's voice jolted her back to the conversation at hand.

"Yes, sorry." She stepped a few feet away and turned her back on Titus for privacy. "He's doing better, but upset, worrying about his coworkers. No one will give me an update on what's happening inside."

"Redman stopped accepting the negotiator's calls."

"That's not good."

"What's not good?" Titus had approached without her noticing.

"Is that Davis?" Mac continued without waiting for confirmation. "Would you mind putting him on?"

"Mac wants to talk to you." She handed Titus the phone but didn't move, eavesdropping on Titus's side of the conversation.

71

"I'm okay. A little shaken." Titus stared into the parking lot, his expression unreadable. "Okay, sure, if you think it will help."

He handed the phone back to Chalissa. She took it, a sense of foreboding permeating her body. "What?"

"The police want to see if Dwayne will talk to Titus," Mac said. "He won't be in any danger, and we insisted you be right beside him, listening to the conversation. But it might give us insight into whether Dwayne is acting on his own…"

She finished the thought for Mac, one that had been bobbing about in her mind. "Or if someone else put him up to it."

# CHAPTER 11

Titus concentrated on the instructions Captain Tanya Stone, the SWAT team negotiator, relayed to him as he glanced through the background information someone had pulled together on Dwayne. Much of it he already knew—he lived alone in the house where he grew up and had worked for Spider Web Designs since the company's inception. But he didn't know Dwayne's father died of pancreatic cancer a decade ago, and his mother of natural causes less than two months later.

"I wasn't born until Mom and Dad were in their early forties," Dwayne had told Titus just a couple of weeks ago. "They had been married for twenty-five years when I arrived. They loved me, but I always had the feeling it was hard to integrate me into their lives."

"Just try to be as natural as possible," Stone concluded. The short, black woman with close-cropped hair had the air of a drill sergeant, albeit one who exuded calm. "We have visual through an air vent in the ceiling, so will be monitoring what Redman is doing as you talk. You'll do fine."

Titus nodded to let her know he heard her, but the advice did nothing to ease the coiled tension riding shotgun in his gut. He adjusted the headset into a more comfortable position over his ears as Chalissa scooted closer in the crowded operations van.

She swung her mic away from her mouth and put her lips near his ear. "You okay?"

Her breath teased his skin, sending promises he shouldn't be filing away to collect on later. He would have to inoculate himself against reading more into her gestures than a professional doing her job at pretending to date him. Although in this context, the law enforcement personnel crammed into the mobile command center knew Chalissa was a U.S. Marshal.

"Titus?"

The concern in her eyes warmed his cold insides even as he'd forgotten her original question. Was it something about whether he was okay? "I'm fine."

"Mr. Davis, we're ready to patch you through," Stone said. "I'll be on the line with you. Remember to look at the screen in front of you—that's where I'll feed you what to say in response to Redman."

Titus glanced at the flat screen. *Relax and breathe* appeared in big block letters. He smiled at the attempt to calm him down. Before he could become any more nervous, Stone patched the call through to the conference room. A ringing phone echoed in Titus's ears. *Please God, let me reach him. Give me the words to say. Keep Dwayne from harming anyone else, including himself.*

"I told you to stop calling me," Dwayne growled.

"Dwayne, it's Titus."

Silence. Titus strained to hear whether the man had disconnected or not. Words flashed on the screen, but he ignored them, going instead with his instinct. "I know you're hurting. It wasn't fair what Jamie did to you, not after all you did to get the company up and running."

"You've got that right," Dwayne said. "Bet he's sorry now."

"I'm sure he is." Titus marshaled his thoughts. "But this isn't the answer."

"No one listens to me!" Frustration dripped from every word

Dwayne said, underlining the turmoil building inside the man with a bomb strapped to his chest. "But they're listening now."

The words on the screen flashed: *Use his name when you talk to him.* "Dwayne, this isn't who you are."

"It's the only way to make them notice me."

From the slight echo buzzing over the line, Titus guessed Dwayne had put the phone on speaker in the conference room. "That's because he doesn't know you like I do. Let me tell him about the Dwayne I know."

Dwayne didn't comment, so Titus spoke from his heart. "The Dwayne I know loaded an injured deer into the back of his car and drove an hour to a wildlife vet. The Dwayne I know plays Santa ever year, traveling to visit the private homes of disabled children who can't get out to see the big man at Christmas."

The soft sound of a snuffle came over the phone line. The negotiator twirled her finger to encourage Titus to continue.

"The Dwayne I know performs hundreds of magic shows at area children's hospitals. Surely, you don't want those kids to hear the man they called Mr. D has blown up a building." Titus let the words hang in the air, hoping the memories of being Mr. D the Magnificent and Santa to those hurting kids would make Dwayne rethink his plan.

"He said this gesture would make them pay for treating me like a worthless piece of garbage," Dwayne said, his voice thick with emotion.

"Who? Who told you that?" Titus could hardly believe someone had pushed Dwayne into this. Had the person done so to try to get Titus killed as collateral damage?

"He tricked me." Anger tinged Dwayne's voice. "He said it was the only way to make my voice heard. But you're right. It was all lies. I was so hurt I believed him. But I didn't want to harm anyone." The sound of crying crackled over the line.

"I know you didn't, Dwayne. There's still time to make it right." Titus read from the screen, glad to have something scripted to say because he had no idea how to respond to such statements on his own. "Will you please disarm the bomb and let your coworkers go?"

Dwayne said something, but his sobs drowned out his words.

"Dwayne, what did you say?"

"The bomb isn't real. I just pretended it was. I'm taking off the vest," Dwayne said. "I'm sorry, I'm so sorry."

On-screen, the conference room door burst open and SWAT team members shouted for Dwayne to raise his hands and get down on his knees. Dwayne complied, tears streaming down his cheeks.

Stone disconnected the call and patted Titus on the shoulder. "You did good."

"Thanks." Titus met Chalissa's gaze. "Who pushed Dwayne into this?"

CHALISSA CHOPPED ONIONS, THEN SLID THEM INTO THE SKILLET TO brown in the heated olive oil. Next she diced a red pepper to add to the skillet. Titus hadn't moved from his seat at the small kitchen table, his shoulders hunched and his hands cupping a mug of hot tea.

She cracked six eggs into a bowl, whisking the yolks before dumping the mixture in with the peppers and onions. Neither one had eaten lunch, and with the clock heading toward five, she had decided omelets would do for an early dinner. To gain more time to recompose himself after the morning's ordeal, Titus had arranged for Sam to spend the afternoon with his classmate, Vanessa Jennings.

After plating their food, she set the plates on the table. "Food's ready." She joined him with her own mug of tea.

"This smells good." He took her hand in his. "Mind if I say a blessing on our food?" He didn't wait for her response but simply bowed his head. "Dear God, thank you for preserving life today."

Chalissa turned her head away from their clasped hands to gaze out the window that overlooked the backyard. A robin hopped onto the deck railing, its red breast puffed out.

"Be with Dwayne," he continued. "Reach his heart and heal the hurt as only you can. Help us to find the answers we need."

How she wished she could believe God would bring them the answers needed, but she'd stopped praying the night Brandon died.

"Keep us safe from harm. Bless this food and the hands that prepared it. Amen."

Titus squeezed her fingers, then released her hand and picked up his fork. If he noticed she hadn't bowed her head to join him in prayer, he gave no indication.

"Hmmm, this is tasty. I had no idea all these ingredients were lurking in my fridge."

She took a bite, not really tasting the omelet. His sincere prayer had jolted her. The way he talked to God as if the "man upstairs" was his friend, his companion, left her with more questions. But she was not going to open that particular box today. Shaking her head, she forked another bite of eggs into her mouth.

He cleared his throat. "A penny for your thoughts."

Concern etched on his features. For a second, she nearly blurted out the truth, that she'd lost her faith in God. Then commonsense returned and she offered a half smile. "Just processing what happened this morning."

His gaze probed hers. To her relief, he accepted the conversational topic. "I can't believe the bomb was fake."

"Well, it could have been real if Dwayne had actually armed it."

"But he didn't." Titus finished his eggs. "Will that help him?"

"In the charges he'll face? Probably, but because no one else knew the bomb wasn't real, it might not matter much." She sipped her cooling tea. "How are you doing?"

He shrugged. "I don't know. I keep thinking I should have picked up on Dwayne's state of mind earlier."

"And done what exactly?"

"Stopped him from strapping a pretend bomb to his chest and taking his coworkers hostage."

"You couldn't have known what he would do."

He ran a hand along his jaw. "He could have been killed or blown himself up."

At the mention of suicide, Chalissa stood and stacked the dishes. She didn't want Titus to notice her discomfort. "You were his friend, but you couldn't control his actions."

Carrying them to the sink, she gazed out the window, fixating on the azalea bushes rimming the left side of the backyard property line. Since her last visit to the Davis residence, the bushes had burst into red, pink, and white flowers, a sign that spring had decided to pull up a chair and stay a while. But interposed over the riot of color and the promise of new life, her brother's face hovered. The last time she saw Brandon, he had been standing beside an azalea bush, its leaves holding faded blooms, his posture slumped and defeated, the hopelessness in his eyes mirroring the hopelessness in her own.

"Who's Brandon?"

The question startled her, breaking into her memories. She must have spoken his name out loud without realizing it. But there was no way she was going to take that particular path down memory lane. Not when she had a witness to convince to move to a safe house. Dwayne's actions might not be directly related to the man outside Sam's window last night, but she couldn't discount Dwayne's mention of a man also.

Since she had to answer Titus's question, she kept her reply succinct. "Brandon is my brother." Turning on the faucet, she rinsed the silverware before loading it into the dishwasher. Memories assailed her, but she pushed through, concentrating on the task at hand.

"You cooked—let me do the dishes." He joined her at the sink.

"I've got it." She stacked the plates into the dishwasher. "Hand me the skillet?"

His fingers brushed hers as she took the cookware, making her even more aware of the attraction she'd tried to deny. Squirting soap into the pan, she added hot water and began to scrub hard, as if she could erase the thoughts now flitting through her mind as easily as the egg residue. If only he weren't hovering beside her, she could more easily ignore his intoxicating presence.

"Do you see Brandon often?"

The skillet slipped from her fingers and clattered in the sink. Picking it up, she rinsed it and put it in the drainer. "No, I don't." Surely, her clipped voice would make him realize the topic of her brother was off limits.

"Where does he live?"

Tears pricked her eyes. She bit her lip to keep them at bay. Sucking in a deep breath, she mumbled, "He's dead."

Titus touched her shoulder. "I'm so sorry, Chalissa."

The compassion in his voice unlocked the tenuous hold she had on her emotions. Tears spilled down her cheeks. Clenching her wet hands, she fought to regain control. His hand slid to her back, rubbing small, soothing circles across her shoulder blades. It had been too long since someone grieved with her over Brandon's death.

"Shhh, I'm here." He turned her body into his, wrapping his arms around her.

For a few seconds, she held herself stiff within the circle of his embrace, not wanting to give into the grief. Then with a sigh, she knotted her hands in his dress shirt and allowed her head to fall onto his chest as the tears flowed. She didn't know how long they stood like that, but eventually, her tears ceased and she simply rested in his arms, the slight sway of their bodies lulling her into a place of peace.

She didn't want to return to reality, not when this alternative felt so good. Reluctantly, she pulled out of his arms. Avoiding his gaze, she moved to the sink and splashed water on her cheeks, drying them with a paper towel.

Her cell rang. "Hey, Mac."

"Just checking in on our witness," Mac said.

"He's doing okay." Hopefully, her voice didn't have a residue of tears in it. She resisted the urge to clear her throat. "Have you found out anything about the man Dwayne said pushed him to blow up his workplace?"

"Not yet. Dwayne had a mental breakdown and had to be sedated. He's at a psychiatric facility for evaluation, but it's unlikely we'll get answers to that question anytime soon."

"Will he be all right?" She had seen some of those facilities and shuddered to think of anyone forced to stay there. "I mean, does it have a good reputation?"

"He'll be in good hands there," Mac said, his voice soft.

"Good to know."

"Have you asked Titus about moving to a safe house?"

She massaged her temple. "Not yet. I'll ask now and call you back."

After disconnecting and relaying what Mac had told her about Dwayne, she said, "We think given what happened with Sam last night and Dwayne today, it would be best if we moved you to a safe house until this is resolved."

Titus shook his head. "Sam doesn't like change."

"You and Sam might not be safe here." Chalissa tried to read his expression, but his face resembled a closed door. She had dealt with stubborn witnesses before, but Titus's intractability got under her skin. Maybe reminding Titus of how his son could react would push him to make the right choice. "Sam will probably not be able to sleep as easily in his room, now that he's had a day to think about what happened last night."

He leaned back against the counter. "The best thing for Sam is to go to sleep in his own bed. If we leave, he will build up the incident to epic proportions and probably never sleep under this roof again."

"But if you don't, you and your son could wind up dead." She hated to put things so starkly, but Titus seemed to be ignoring the obvious.

Titus crossed his arms. "Are you saying the Marshals can't keep us safe?"

# CHAPTER 12

The more Titus thought about what happened the night before, the more he became convinced his son had embellished the story. As he'd told Chalissa the night before, Sam told the truth as a rule, but lately he'd begun spinning tall tales. Maybe reading *The Invention of Hugo Cabret* hadn't been such a good idea after all.

Still, Titus regretted crossing swords with Chalissa. Nonetheless, he wouldn't put his son's future in jeopardy because of a harmless prank.

"Dad!" Sam burst into the kitchen, his backpack bouncing in place.

Titus had never been so glad of his son's interruption than now. At least he could focus on something other than Chalissa's stormy eyes.

"Titus?" Barbara Jennings called from the front stoop.

"Is it six thirty already?" Titus glanced at the stove clock. "I was supposed to pick Sam up from the Jennings ten minutes ago." He hurried to the open front door and stepped outside to join Barbara. "I'm so sorry, I completely lost track of time."

Barbara wagged a key fob at him. "I tried to call you but kept getting your voicemail."

He reached into his front shirt pocket for his phone. Dead. "Sorry, I didn't realize it needed charging."

"I'm just toying with you." She fluttered her eyelashes up at Titus. "I have to get Vanessa to her ballet lesson." Her daughter waved from the back seat of the Honda Pilot parked at the curb.

A whiff of something cloying teased his nostrils and he barely managed to hold back a sneeze. Why did some women wear such strong perfume? Chalissa smelled of lavender and fresh air, an appealing combination that brought a smile.

"Titus?" Barbara cocked her head.

He'd missed whatever she had said before his name. "Sorry, my thoughts wandered."

Her brow furrowed. "I asked if you and Sam wanted to come to dinner Friday night."

"Friday night?" He rubbed the back of his neck as he raced to come up with an excuse. He'd tried in the past to politely spell out he wasn't interested in moving their relationship past friendship, but Barbara remained oblivious.

"I'm sorry," he began, then realized it was the third or fourth time he'd apologized to her in the space of five minutes. "I seem to be saying that a lot lately."

"Seems that way."

"Thank you for asking, but I have an engagement on Friday night." That sounded stilted but hopefully it didn't leave any wiggle room.

"How about Saturday night instead?" The optimistic look in the divorcee's eyes made Titus realize he'd been doing Barbara a disservice by not being direct about his disinterest.

Time to stop pussyfooting around, as his grandfather used to say. "Barbara, I appreciate your invitation." A smile blossomed across her face, and he hated that what he'd say next would stamp it out. "I'm not interested in dating you."

Her expression fell. "Why not? Is it me?"

How do you tell a woman you don't find her attractive? No man on earth had ever figured out how to do that without causing a lot of heartache. "It's just that—"

"He likes Ms. Manning." Sam squeezed beside him on the porch, angling his head up to his dad. "Isn't that right?"

Titus wasn't fooled for a minute by the innocent look in his son's eyes, but he did thank God for Sam's impeccable timing. "I, er—" Before he could formulate exactly how to respond to his son's declaration, Sam continued.

"So he can't go out with you." Sam shifted his gaze to Barbara. "Because he's taking Ms. Manning to dinner on Friday *and* Saturday."

Apparently, Sam had his weekend all planned out. Titus would talk to his son about his presumption.

"I see." Barbara clearly didn't, if Titus interpreted her furrowed brow correctly.

"Everything okay?" Chalissa joined them on the porch. She placed a hand on Sam's shoulder, her face neutral.

"Yes," Titus said. He turned to Barbara. "Do you remember Chalissa Manning from Burke Lake? Chalissa, Barbara Jennings."

"You have a little girl Sam's age," Chalissa said, her voice and posture relaxed. Maybe she'd realized he wasn't going to move to a safe house and had decided not to push things after all.

"Vanessa and Sam are great friends." Barbara narrowed her eyes as she looked at Chalissa—she probably didn't view the Marshal like Titus did.

His late wife had a thick mass of black, curly hair she'd worn long. Chalissa's short, straight hair framed her face perfectly. Maybe on their date Friday night, he'd get another chance to touch it. If he could talk her into actually going out with him. On a pretend date that he wished wasn't pretend.

Barbara laid a hand on Titus's arm. "If you happen to have a free evening, give me a call. Like I said, I've got to get Vanessa to ballet."

"Thanks again for letting Sam hang out after school today." Titus watched Barbara get into her car and drive away before he turned back to the pair standing in the foyer. Since he couldn't very well make his son a liar, he said to Chalissa before she could bring up the previous topic, "Would you like to go to dinner Friday evening? I've been meaning to try Curry Mantra, if you like Indian food."

For a moment, he thought she would refuse. Then she simply said, "I'd love to, although I admit to not liking really spicy food."

"They have a good mix of spicy and not-so-spicy foods." Titus ruffled Sam's hair. "I'll find a sitter for Sam and pick you up at seven on Friday."

TURNING ON THE TAPS FOR THE JACUZZI TUB, CHALISSA FILLED IT WITH hot water, then sprinkled in eucalyptus and tea bath salts. She'd managed to get out of work at five on the dot, giving her time to have a relaxing bath before Titus arrived for their date. Mac had told her not to fight Titus on the move to a safe house—better to have the witness cooperating in a place they could keep an eye on than disgruntled and more prone to make mistakes in a location they didn't want to be.

Which meant, for tonight at least, she could pretend she was getting ready for a real date. How long had it been since she was this excited about a date? For that matter, how long had it been since she'd gone out with a man? Too long. Her job didn't allow for much down time and most of the men she did meet found her work hours difficult to accommodate a relationship. To be honest, no one had made her want to adjust her schedule.

She leaned her head against the bath pillow, letting the jets do their magic. Closing her eyes, she mentally sorted through her wardrobe for what to wear. Curry Mantra wasn't an upscale restaurant, so she didn't need to dress up too much. Perhaps the sapphire blue raw silk top with three-quarter sleeves paired with the dark brown pencil skirt that ended just above her knees. Light brown, knee-high leather boots with her grandmother's silk shawl would keep her warm enough on the cool April evening.

Her outfit decided, Chalissa allowed herself a few moments to dwell on Titus, not as a witness, but as a man. Maybe she'd get a chance to see if his beard was scruffy or soft. She'd been longing to find out since they'd first met. His gentleness in dealing with Sam and the tenderness she'd felt when he'd held her in his arms as she cried over Brandon filled her with a warm fuzzy feeling. She shook her head. This wasn't a real date—she shouldn't be mooning over the man.

Wrapped in a towel, she applied lotion to her face. Humming a tune that had been rattling around in her brain for a few days, she paused as the lyrics came to her. *This is the day the Lord has made.* It had been years since she'd thought of that song, but what's learned in childhood did indeed stick with you for a lifetime. Her first foster family had taken her to church regularly and she'd believed God could help reunite her and Brandon in a loving family. But as the years passed and she bounced from her father's home to other foster families while Brandon languished in group homes, she mentally boxed up all thoughts of God.

The memory now reminded her of why she couldn't have a future with Titus, even if he testified and could leave witness protection. It was clear God was an integral part of his and Sam's life. While part of her appreciated how comforting that must be after all the Davis family had been through, she certainly wasn't ready to forgive or forget what God had allowed to happen to her and Brandon.

All at once the thought of meeting Titus for dinner at an Indian restaurant knotted her stomach. She shouldn't have agreed to the evening out, even if it made their "relationship" seem genuine to Sam. Tonight, she would stay professional, despite longing to have an actual date with the handsome man she'd been daydreaming about for days.

# CHAPTER 13

Titus parked the car and flipped down the visor to check to see if he had anything stuck in his teeth. Nope, his pearly whites looked good. His nerves jangled as he walked across the parking lot to Chalissa's apartment. He passed a few other young professionals on the outside stairs of the garden-style apartment building. Her unit sat at the back corner on the top floor of the three-story structure. At number 306, he rapped on the door, then smoothed his hair. *Not a real date.* Maybe if he repeated the phrase enough in his head, he'd act less like a teenager about to go on his first date.

He knocked again. This time, the clink of a chain being dragged and a deadbolt unlocking greeted his knock. The door opened a crack, allowing him to glimpse Chalissa's right eye and little else.

"I'm running late. Would you count to ten, then come in while I finish getting dressed?"

"Okay."

She closed the door and he dutifully counted to ten before entering her apartment. After relocking the handle, he moved into the living/dining room combination and stopped short. A modest-sized flat screen TV hung on the far wall opposite the kitchen area, which boasted a bar counter and two stools. Instead of a couch, a folded treadmill stood in front of the TV, with a large bean bag chair to the right. Sliding glass doors with closed venetian blinds indicated the apartment had a balcony.

"Not quite what you expected."

He turned to see Chalissa standing at the edge of the hallway leading back to what he presumed would be a bedroom and bathroom. "The furnishings are unique."

She waved a hand in a circular motion. "This is temporary. I've only lived here three months, and I always like to get a feel for the area before I find a permanent place to live. So most of my stuff is in storage—no sense moving twice."

"I see where your priorities are." He pointed to the TV and treadmill.

She laughed. "I do enjoy a good binge watching while I exercise. Are you ready?"

"Yes." He allowed himself to take a good look at her as she went ahead of him to the door. She wore a blue top with a short straight skirt and knee-high leather boots with a shawl looped over one arm. When she paused at the door to glance back at him, he said, "You look lovely."

Her brown eyes widened. "Thank you."

Once in the car, she asked about Sam, and he related a story about his son's attempt to get out of homework that made Chalissa smile. He could get used to her smiles. At the restaurant, which was packed on a Friday night, a hostess wearing a bright purple sari led them through to the second dining room. On a small stage, a man played what the website had billed as traditional Indian music on a sitar.

The hostess stopped at a table for two at the end of a long bench seat that serviced one side of a row of tables. "Your server will be with you shortly. Enjoy your meal."

"Would you like the booth or the chair?" Titus said.

"I'll take the booth side." She slid onto the seat opposite him, settling her shawl and purse beside her. "This place is charming."

"The food's good too." He caught a glimpse of himself in one of the strategically placed mirrors interspersed with pictures of India that created the impression of a much larger space. His overeager expression made him inwardly wince. *Calm down, Davis.*

She opened her menu. "Good to know."

After placing their orders, Titus sipped his water. "I feel like I'm at a bit of a disadvantage."

"Oh?"

"You know all about me, but I know very little about you."

"There's not much to tell."

"How about the basics?"

"Fair enough." She laid her napkin in her lap. "I'm thirty-four, never been married. My mom died when I was eight. I like baseball but tend to throw my allegiance behind the home team of where I'm currently living—go Nationals! I love camping and hiking. Being in nature seems to be so restorative to my soul."

"So your father raised you?"

A shadow passed across her face. "In a way."

"And Brandon?" He shouldn't push her about her brother, but curiosity drove him to ask. He'd been curious to learn more ever since she'd cried in his arms.

Chalissa straightened, her gaze directed to the tablecloth. "Brandon was two years older than me. He was different as a kid, but my parents kept thinking he'd outgrow it—but they never bothered to figure out what 'it' was. He didn't get diagnosed with autism until he was twelve."

"You mentioned he had died. What happened?"

Her eyes met his, the pain in hers reflecting what had been in his heart a thousand times over Sam's struggles. "He eventually was put in a group home with other troubled kids, and he died when I was seventeen."

"I'm so sorry. That must have been very difficult." Titus covered her hand with his. Before he could say more, their server stopped by their table bearing a tray.

"Here is your chicken tikka masala." The waiter put the dish near

Chalissa's plate. "And your butter chicken." He arranged Titus's dishes in front of him. "And rice to share. Enjoy."

"Thank you." Titus offered the rice bowl to Chalissa. "Please, you go first."

While they ate, Titus kept the conversation light, discussing the usual first date topics of movies, books, and music. They decided to share gulab jamun, a dessert of homemade milk balls dipped in honey-sugar syrup, along with coffee.

"How did you meet your late wife?" Chalissa stirred cream into her coffee.

"My turn to be in the hot seat?" Titus sampled one of the milk balls.

"Something like that."

"Believe it or not, it was while I was smoothing concrete for a sidewalk."

"You worked construction?" She cocked her head. "I didn't peg you as the construction-worker type."

He wagged a finger at her. "Looks can be deceiving. It's how I put myself through college. Paid well and allowed me to spend a lot of time outside." He'd liked the satisfaction of working with his hands, of the camaraderie of the other men—and a few women—on his crew. "My dad was a master stonecutter. He had his own business, building retaining walls, garden walkways, fire pits, that sort of thing. I worked for him since I was a kid, carrying stones and learning how to fit them together."

"You must miss him."

He'd forgotten she would have known about his parents' death in a car accident when he was a freshman in college. "I do."

"Why didn't you follow in his footsteps with stonemasonry?"

"I didn't have his ability to design. I could follow directions, but I couldn't create something from scratch. My parents weren't well off. They had modest life insurance policies and a mortgage. When their estate was settled, there wasn't a lot left to pay for my education." He shrugged. "Hence the construction work."

"You sound like you enjoyed it." She snagged the last milk ball, dipping it in the syrup before popping it into her mouth.

"I did. It was hot, dirty work most of the time. But it felt honest, and it turned out to be pretty good therapy too." And it had been. Hauling eighty-pound bags of concrete around all day required little mental energy but tired him out physically so that he slept most nights.

He returned to her original question about how he'd met Eve. "I continued working construction as much as I could while taking accounting classes. When I graduated, I had a hard time initially finding a new position, so worked construction full-time while juggling some part-time bookkeeping for a few small businesses in the evenings. The construction company had a city contract to replace aging sidewalks in the business district, so I had been checking the freshly poured concrete for bubbles, smoothing out any ripples, when she walked by."

He could still smell the cloying scent of Eve's perfume.

"What, you catcalled her?" Chalissa's eyes narrowed.

"Me? No way. I'm not the kind of man who would whistle at a woman, no matter how attractive." Titus grimaced. "Thankfully, the crew I worked on had too much respect for women. No, she was skirting the sidewalk in the gutter when a bicyclist blew past her and must have knocked into her, because the next thing I knew, she was falling toward the wet cement."

Even telling the story kicked his heart rate up a notch. He'd leaped over the cement to the curb, managing to catch her arm in time to prevent her landing on the smooth, sticky surface.

"So you rescued her from tumbling into the cement?"

He nodded.

"Aw, that's such a meet-cute. You should send your story in to those TV channels that do all the romance movies—there's only so much coffee that can be spilled onto the hero or heroine in their first meeting."

If only the rest of their story had conformed to a romantic movie plot, he might not be here. But, for Sam's sake, he tried to hold onto the good times.

"I bet Sam loves that story."

"I don't know if I've told him." He shrugged. "But you're right—he would enjoy hearing it."

After paying the bill, Titus glanced at his watch. "Ready? I told the sitter we'd be back by nine."

"It's eight thirty already?" Chalissa gathered her purse and shawl.

"I guess the adage 'Time flies when you're having fun' is true." He cupped her elbow as they threaded their way through the tables and exited the restaurant. Without analyzing his reasons, he slid his hand down her forearm and linked his fingers with hers. Chalissa gave him a quick smile before turning her gaze toward the parking lot.

Her body tensed beside him. Dropping his hand, she stepped in front of him. "Get back in the restaurant and wait there." With a push on his shoulder, she turned him toward the entrance.

"What do you see?" He craned his neck to look over his shoulder, but she used her shoulder to move him backwards.

"Check in with the sitter and stay inside until I come get you." Her voice jolted him into action. Entering the restaurant, his thoughts turned to Sam. He dialed the sitter's cell and prayed his son was safe.

As soon as Titus disappeared into the restaurant, Chalissa called one of the Marshals sitting outside the Davis home. "It's Chalissa. How are things there?"

"Quiet. Some traffic, but all either kept driving down the street or pulled into the driveway of a house on the block. We've taken turns walking the perimeter of the house every fifteen minutes, but nothing suspicious," Inspector Susan Burlington said. "What's happening on your end?"

"Someone smashed the taillights of his SUV while we were in the restaurant. I sent him back inside while I check it out. With the courthouse threat and the incident with Sam a few nights ago, not to mention the averted hostage situation at Titus's workplace, she wasn't taking any chances.

"I'll stick close to the house. Do you want me to send backup to the restaurant?"

"Not quite yet. I don't want to overreact and blow our dating cover. But if I don't send you a text in five minutes, call it in." That would allow her time to assess the situation and still keep Titus safe.

"Will do."

"Thanks, Susan." Chalissa disconnected the call and walked to the parking spot where Titus had parked his SUV a row away from the restaurant's entrance. She scanned the area around the vehicle but saw no one. Red plastic littered the ground near the bumper. Her eyes flicked to the cars on either side of the SUV. The vehicle on the left had at least one broken taillight as well.

A couple in their twenties crossed behind the SUV before Chalissa could warn them about the debris. The woman's high-heeled boot crunched on the broken plastic, her left ankle twisting. "Oh!" she cried as she stumbled into her companion.

Chalissa hurried forward as the man caught the woman, righting her. "Are you okay?"

The young woman glanced down at the scattered shards of plastic, then at the busted taillights. "I think so, but look at what happened to this car."

The man, his arm around his companion, leaned closer to Titus's SUV. "Someone got both lights. Must be the same crew that's been hitting cars in the neighborhood."

Chalissa checked out the car to the left. Both taillights had been shattered. "There's been similar vandalism in the area?"

The man nodded. "We live over there," he gestured to the left, indicating the houses next to the shopping strip. "Last week, someone broke the lights on half a dozen vehicles on our street alone. The cops said they've received a bunch of calls about car damage. They think it's some teenagers having fun."

Chalissa used her camera phone to snap a photo of the damage to Titus's car.

"That your car?" The man pointed to Titus's SUV.

"Yes," Chalissa said.

"Good luck," the man said before walking with the woman toward the restaurant.

Chalissa sent a quick text to Susan, indicating backup wasn't needed but asking she send the police to the restaurant to file a report. Chalissa texted Titus to hang on for a few more minutes, then she quickly walked through the parking lot to ensure no other danger was present. She discovered seven more vehicles with smashed taillights. While the evidence of other cars having similar damage seemed to indicate it had nothing to do with Titus, the timing made her unsettled, as if she were missing something. A police car pulled into the parking lot. Time to retrieve Titus and file a report with the cop.

Forty minutes later, Titus parked at her apartment complex. "Well, that wasn't exactly how I thought the evening would end."

"Me, either." She inwardly groaned as she factored in the paperwork related to the vandalism. Not her favorite part of the job, but she understood the importance of filing reports for any unusual incident related to one of her witnesses.

"Do you think the police will catch whoever did all that damage?"

"Maybe." She reached for the SUV door handle. "Thank you for dinner. I'll see myself up."

"My mom taught me to always see my date home, not the parking lot." Before she could object, he was out of the car and circling the hood to open her door.

She slid out to stand beside him on the asphalt. His hand warmed the small of her back as they moved to the sidewalk, where she halted behind his vehicle. "But since this wasn't a real date, you don't have to walk me upstairs." She glanced around the lot. "I know the police think the vehicle damage was tied to the other incidents, but the whole thing makes me uneasy."

Titus hesitated. "If you're sure..."

"I insist." She made a shooing motion with her hand.

Instead of returning to the driver's side door, he leaned over and kissed her cheek. "Real date or not, I enjoyed spending time with you."

Then he was off, leaving her to stare after the broken taillights and wonder how on earth she was going to keep a professional distance from Titus when her heart longed to cross the friendship line.

# CHAPTER 14

"First, you grab a worm." Titus selected one worm from the bait container and held it up for Sam to see. The lake water glistened in the late afternoon sun, the temperature soaring near eighty degrees. While maybe not the perfect time of day, the need to relax on the pier with his son and a fishing pole in his hands had been enough for Titus.

"Dad, I want to try it!" Sam wiggled nearly as much as the worm twisting in Titus's fingers.

"Sure, but be careful you don't let it go." He handed it to Sam, who promptly dropped it into the water.

"Oh, no." Sam's upper lip trembled. "It's gone."

Titus pointed to the full bait container. "Don't worry—we have plenty. Get another one from the tub."

Ten minutes later, half of the worms from the tub had been fed to the fish, with none making it onto the hook at the end of Sam's fishing pole. With every dropped worm, Sam's frustration level grew along with his determination to spear a worm on the hook.

When yet another worm slipped out of his fingers and into the lake, Sam threw down his pole. "I don't wanna fish. This is stupid!"

Tears sprang to his eyes. Titus read in his son's watery expression a deeper fear, that this was another thing he couldn't do.

"It's okay, we can just sit for a while and look at the water." Titus wanted to say more, but had learned to keep his comments short until Sam calmed down.

"Is there room for one more?" Chalissa approached with a smile, a battered fishing pole and tackle box in her hands.

Titus rose. "Hi, sure. How'd you..." He swallowed the rest of the question. Of course she knew where he and Sam were—the Marshals were keeping close tabs on them. With Sam staring at him, he recovered with, "It's nice to see you."

She cocked her head. "You didn't think I'd let you catch all the fish, did you? I'm hungry for a fried fish dinner."

Sam's eyes widened. "You like to fish?"

Chalissa dropped to the pier beside Sam's chair, letting her feet dangle over the edge. "Who doesn't like to fish?" She set her tackle box down and leaned around Sam to eye the bait tub. "Hmmm, have you caught anything?"

"Nothing. I can't get the worm on the hook." His slumped posture and dejected voice spoke loud and clear.

Chalissa met Titus's gaze, then nudged Sam with her elbow. "Hey, do you want to know the secret to getting a worm on the hook?"

Sam turned his head sideways and looked at her. "There's a secret?"

"Yep." Reaching around Sam, she took the bait container and moved it closer to her. "First, you should keep your worms cool."

"Why?" Sam fastened his gaze on Chalissa's face.

Titus contented himself with watching the pair interact as Chalissa explained that the cold kept the worms less wiggly and mushy. She then took Sam's hand and led him down the pier to the edge of the parking lot to rub dirt on their hands. His son laughed and clapped his hands together, sending puffs of dust into the air.

An older man, wearing a round fishing hat decorated with lures and holding a pole in his hand, halted beside Titus's chair. "That's a fine family you've got there. Not many mothers are willing to get their hands dirty to fish."

"I, uh," Titus ditched any effort to explain and settled on agreement, his eyes on Chalissa. "Yes, she's pretty amazing."

The older man laughed. "It does my old heart good to see you're still smitten with your missus. I had forty-five good years with mine." He cleared his throat. "You should tell her every day how much you love her, young man."

"I will." Titus nodded. He couldn't help but grin as the man walked away whistling the theme song to "The Andy Griffith Show." He'd watched many an episode with his granddad as a boy and had learned to whistle that same tune. His late wife hated it when he'd inadvertently whistled the song around the house, but then again, toward the end, she hadn't liked anything he'd done.

"Dad, look!" Sam thrust his hands in front of Titus, reeling him out of his bittersweet memories. "Miss Chalissa said the dirt will help the worms not be as scared when we pick them up."

"Is that so?" Titus raised his eyebrows as Chalissa dropped down onto the pier.

"Oh, yes. Worms have a good sense of smell." She plucked a worm from the container. "Besides, it gives you extra grip."

Sam dropped into his chair beside her. "Here's my hook."

"Okay, now you put a tiny cut into the worm." She demonstrated with a pocket knife. Sam's attention never strayed from her explanation on how to slide the worm onto the hook.

Titus turned his gaze to the lake. Several boats had dropped anchor toward the center while a couple in a canoe paddled near the shoreline and a trio of kayakers struck out toward the opposite side of the water.

A rowboat packed with four teenage boys drifted toward the small island roughly in the lake's center. The teens splashed at each other, their raucous behavior sending the boat rocking. One of them pointed to something on the Vesper Island State Waterfowl Refuge.

"A tug!" Sam jumped up from his chair, excitement making his body quiver all over. "I got something!"

Chalissa rose to stand behind Sam, her hands closing over his to steady the pole. "Yeah, it looks like you hooked something. Now we bring it in nice and slow." She looked over Sam's head to Titus. "Would you ready the net for our catch?"

"Sure." As Titus bent to pick up the handle of their small fishing net, something exploded in the water a few feet away.

CHALISSA DIDN'T THINK—SHE SIMPLY ACTED. KNOCKING THE POLE from Sam's grasp, she hauled the boy behind her, shoving him down as she bent her body over his. Titus crouched beside her and she shifted her stance to cover them both.

Another explosion sent water into the air, along with a few fish.

She reached for her weapon. Laughter drew her attention over her shoulder to the lake, where the rowboat with the four teens had drifted closer to the dock.

One teen pointed to the water, where fish floated. "Did you see how high the water shot up?" His comment set off another round of guffaws from his boat mates. Another teen leaned over the side of the boat with a net and scooped up the dead fish.

Some of the tension eased between Chalissa's shoulders. Just some teens using dynamite to "fish," although where they got the dynamite made her suspicious.

"Let's try another." The first teenager held a stick of dynamite in his hand.

"Gentlemen, dock your boat," a man's voice, projected by a bull-horn, pierced the air. A police motorboat zoomed up behind the teens with a pair of officers.

"Busted!" a second teen said, followed by more laughter. His demeanor changed as the police boat sidled up next to the rowboat.

Chalissa slowly straightened as the officers talked to the teens. The rowboat with the four teens rocked as one managed to fit the oars into the riggers and pull in the direction of the dock, the police right behind them. She tapped Titus on his shoulder. "It's okay. Those bozos were trying to fish with dynamite."

"I thought that was an urban myth," Titus said, his hand resting on Sam's shoulder.

"It's illegal in Virginia, but that doesn't stop people from trying it," she said. "But dynamite is hard to come by, so I wonder where those boys got hold of several sticks."

Nathan Wiltshire, the park employee who'd helped when Sam had gone missing, walked up the pier toward them. "Everyone okay?"

Sam wrapped his arms around Chalissa's waist in a tight grip. "That was scary."

"Yes, it was." Wiltshire watched the boys bring the rowboat alongside the dock. "I'm just glad no one got hurt."

"The fish got hurt." Sam pointed to the water, where several dead fish floated. "That's not how you're supposed to catch fish."

"It's definitely not." Wiltshire nodded at Chalissa and Titus, then strode off to meet the teens as they clambered onto the end of the dock. The police officers joined Wiltshire, forming a knot around the teens.

"Are you okay, Sam?" Titus kneeled down in front of Sam.

"I wanted to catch a fish, but I lost my pole."

Chalissa's heart constricted. She'd reacted to the threat on instinct, Sam's fishing pole forgotten in her haste to keep him and his father safe. Now that the threat had passed, she leaned slightly over the edge of the pier to see if she could spot the pole.

"Looking for this?" A man wearing dry hip waders held a dripping pole in his hand.

"My fishing pole!" Sam clapped his hands. "You found it."

"Here you go." The man handed the pole to Sam and waved off Chalissa and Titus's thanks. "I saw what happened." He shook his head as the police and Wiltshire marshaled the now subdued group of teens down the pier.

Chalissa detected a whiff of beer as they passed. Alcohol often fueled stupidity, especially in those under the legal age to imbibe. She pulled out her phone and sent a text to the office for someone to follow up with the police to find out where the dynamite came from and if someone cajoled the teens into the prank. She exchanged a glance with Titus, then tugged on Sam's sleeve to get his attention. "I think the fish have had enough excitement for today."

His face fell. "No more fishing?"

"Another time. Really." She tousled his hair as Sam sighed, then put the lid back on the bait container. After helping Titus and Sam pack up, she buckled Sam into the car.

"You won't forget?" Sam adjusted his glasses.

"About fishing again? No way." She winked at him, her gesture triggering a smile from Titus in the front seat. His eyes crinkled, highlighting laugh lines that would deepen over time. A sudden vision of Titus at sixty, silver hair and more pronounced wrinkles on his still-handsome face, filled her mind. She blinked and, with a final wave, watched the pair drive off, their Marshal tail behind them.

She had no business thinking of a future with this man and his son, but that didn't stop her from longing to have one—despite the fact that someone was out to end his life.

# CHAPTER 15

The next evening, Chalissa juggled the restaurant carryout bag, laptop case, and purse as she exited her vehicle. She nodded to the Marshals in their car curbside in front of the Davis home. Her shoulders relaxed a fraction at the thought of their keeping watch while she was inside with Titus and Sam.

Titus pulled open the door before she made it halfway up the walk. "Hi."

Sam peered around his father, his hair sticking up as if he'd slept on it wet. "Dad said you were bringing us dinner. I'm hungry."

She hefted the food bag. "Yep, from Hamrocks down the street." She shifted her focus to Titus. "They have a family dinner takeout special."

The Davis men stepped back to let her enter the house and Titus closed the door behind her.

Sam trotted beside her as she made her way to the kitchen. "It smells good. What is it?"

"One of my favorites. Penne pasta with marinara sauce, parmesan, and meatballs."

Sam's eyes lit up. "I love meatballs!"

"Plus fresh broccoli, a Caesar salad, and garlic bread." She set the food on the counter.

"*Ugh*, salad and broccoli." Sam made a face.

She smiled at the boy, then handed him her laptop case. "Put this in the living room for me, and I'll tell you the special surprise I got for us."

"Okay. But I'm not eating broccoli." He took the case and trudged over to the coffee table.

"Not his favorite veggie," Titus said. He got out three plates and silverware while she unpacked their dinner.

"I think we can persuade him to eat some for this." Chalissa waited until Sam had come back to the kitchen. "Ready for the surprise?"

He nodded. "What is it?"

"This." She drew the final box from the bag and held it out to Sam. "Will you do the honors?"

A frown puckered his face. "What does that mean?"

"Oh, it means will you open the box to show the surprise." She waited while he carefully removed the piece of tape holding the lid down, then raised the top.

"It's chocolate cake. My favorite." He reached inside the box, but she playfully snapped it closed on his fingers before he could take a swipe at the frosting.

Chalissa whisked the box away and put it on top of the fridge. "That's what awaits you if you manage to eat your dinner," she leaned closer to Sam, "and your broccoli."

"No fair," Sam stomped his foot, but his father laid a hand on his shoulder. "Sorry."

Titus handed Sam the plates and silverware. "Why don't you set the table?"

"Okay," Sam said, then carried the stack over to the table.

"Think he'll eat the broccoli?" Chalissa picked up the pasta container.

Titus grabbed the veggie and salad dishes. "For chocolate cake? You betcha."

Sam dominated the conversation during dinner, chattering on about how he and two of his classmates had built an elaborate marble run during Innovation Space time at school. Chalissa was thankful for the distraction. At least he wasn't fixated on their interrupted fishing yesterday afternoon. And Sam hadn't commented on the SUV sitting outside their house with two Marshals inside.

While he talked, Sam ate his one piece of broccoli and micro-bite of salad. Seeing him enjoy his cake made her smile. After polishing off his piece of cake, Sam lifted his plate to his mouth, tongue extended.

"Put the plate down—you're done with the cake." Titus sounded stern, but the wink he sent Chalissa showed he found the gesture amusing.

Chalissa smiled, then took the remains of the cake to the kitchen. Brandon used to do that exact same thing whenever he had a piece of cake. An image of her brother sitting at the kitchen table enthusiastically licking the plate after his ninth birthday while their father and his latest girlfriend screamed at each other flashed in her mind. That had been the last birthday celebration they'd shared as a family.

At the sink, she rinsed the knife used to cut the cake, then started loading the dishwasher.

"You don't have to do the dishes." Titus set down the stack of dessert plates, then touched her shoulder. "Are you okay?"

"Just thinking of Brandon. He used to lick the plate after cake too." She added the dessert plates to the dishwasher.

"You must miss him." The compassion behind the statement knocked her off balance.

"I do. When my mom died, my dad just left. I managed to land in a decent foster home, but Brandon ended up in a group home for troubled kids. My foster family helped me visit him as often as I could, but Brandon hated it there." She swallowed the lump filling her throat. The desire to share more than the bare bones of her story—to share a piece of herself—with this kind man overcame her reticence. Maybe once she did, the hole in her heart wouldn't feel quite so big.

She turned off the water and dried her hands. "When I was a

senior, I started making plans for Brandon to come live with me after I graduated. I had such dreams of the two of us setting up house. Brandon had gotten a job as a grocery bagger at a local supermarket, and I would find work as well and take classes at the community college." She sighed, memories of those days crowding into her mind. "I really thought we could make it work."

"But Brandon didn't think so?"

"He said he did, but," she looked away, the words lodging in her throat, "the day we were to go look at apartments, I arrived at the group home to pick him up. No one knew where he was at first. Then someone said they'd seen him walking toward the edge of the property where a stand of trees stood."

"I'm so sorry." Titus hauled her into his arms.

With her head against his chest, she managed to get the rest of the tale told. "He had found a rope and hanged himself. I learned later that a couple of the residents had teased him mercilessly, and his note said he simply couldn't take it anymore."

He rubbed her back, the motion soothing away some of the hurt.

"It was tough, especially since I wasn't old enough to push for an investigation into what had driven him to suicide and my dad didn't care." She shuddered as a memory from Brandon's funeral gripped her thoughts. "Do you know what my father said to me when we buried my brother? 'At least he did one good thing for me by dying when he did.'"

"What did he mean by that?"

She pulled back from his embrace. "Dear old dad had taken out a life insurance policy on Brandon and he needed the money to pay off debts. I think he probably had one on me too. Who thinks of their child's death as a good thing?"

"That must have really hurt to hear what was inside his heart."

"You have no idea." Just thinking of her dad drove away the last vestiges of tears. "Then my father had the gall to say that Brandon's in a better place." She snorted. "If God cared that much about Brandon to let him into heaven, why hadn't he taken better care of my brother on earth?"

THE PAIN IN CHALISSA'S EYES REMINDED HIM OF HIS OWN ANGUISH when he'd discovered Eve's infidelity and cancer diagnosis on the same day. "I don't have all the answers, but what I do know is that God's ways are not our ways."

"So we're just supposed to leave everything in God's capable hands?"

He inwardly winced at the sarcasm in her tone, but chose to address the hurt behind her words. "In a word? Yes."

She stared at him. "But—"

Titus held up his hand. "May I continue before you offer a counterargument?"

"Sure, go ahead." She crossed her arms and leaned back against the counter.

"Let me make sure Sam's getting into his PJs." He hurried down the hall to his son's bedroom and peeked in. Sam had his shirt off and was working on getting his shoes untied. Titus slipped back to the kitchen. "I don't want him to overhear this. When Eve received her cancer diagnosis, she was so angry that she confided she'd been having an affair." It never got any easier saying those words out loud.

"Apparently, she'd been seeing this other man for nearly our entire marriage." He'd never suspected her encouraging him to work overtime had less to do with the extra money and more to do with an easy way to cuckhold him. "You could say God and I had words about that."

"That must have been rough." Her eyes softened some, but her stance didn't alter.

"Throughout her treatment, she'd taunt me with stories of what they'd done together, but to my knowledge, he never visited her in the hospital or tried to get in touch with her." Now for the really difficult part. "When it became apparent she was dying, she told me she wasn't sure if Sam was mine."

"That's terrible." Her arms relaxed. "I can see why that would make you angry at God."

"It did, for a time." He spread his hands. "But then I realized just who I was angry at. It wasn't some fallible human, but the infallible Almighty God, maker of heaven and earth. His ways are indeed higher than my ways, as the prophet Isaiah says."

"You're saying that because God is God, we shouldn't question why he allows certain things to happen?"

"Not exactly. I'm saying that because God is God, we don't have the full picture—we only have our tiny piece of the puzzle. And because we don't know how our piece fits into the whole, we can't determine how Brandon or Eve's life fit into it."

Her brow furrowed. "I'm not sure that makes sense."

"I'm ready for bed!" Sam hopped from one foot to the other in his pajamas. "Miss Chalissa, you said you'd read me another chapter in my book."

"I did indeed. Shall we sit in the living room?"

"Sure." Sam raced off.

Chalissa followed him, pausing in the doorway. "Thanks for listening."

"Anytime." As he finished the dishes, he prayed for Chalissa. *God, please heal her heart and draw her back to you.*

"I LIKE HER, DAD." SAM DREW THE COVERS UNDER HIS CHIN.

Titus didn't pretend to not understand what his son meant. "I know."

"She doesn't try to be extra nice to me because she likes you, either." Sam's sleepy eyes fixed on Titus. "She acts like she likes me."

"That she does," Titus agreed. "Now good night, Sam." He moved to the door and flicked off the light.

"Dad, do you think Mom would have liked her?"

The question caught Titus off-guard as he stood in the doorway, his hand on the knob. In the semi-darkness, he couldn't read Sam's expression, but he still caught the yearning in his son's voice. Eve would have turned her nose up at Chalissa's ease with a fishing pole and bait, her athleticism. His late wife was the epitome of a girly-girl, never one to muss her hair or manicure. Chalissa regularly kept her hair under a battered baseball cap and her nails were short and polish-free. No, Eve wouldn't have given Chalissa Manning the time of day, but that was something his son wouldn't hear from him.

Instead, he settled on an answer that skirted the truth. "Probably."

Sam didn't reply, and Titus quietly shut the door. In the hallway, he leaned the back of his head against the wall as thoughts of Eve running roughshod over him crowded his mind. It was getting harder and harder to remember the early days when they both were so happy together. Now he could only recall her beautiful face twisted in rage at his missing yet another cultural event she deemed "must see" due to his long workdays. No matter how hard he tried to meet her demands, he came up short.

"Titus?"

Chalissa's query from the other end of the hallway jolted him back to the present. Straightening, he walked toward her. "Sorry. Got caught up in the past." The guilt at how things had ended between him and Eve warred with the relief he sometimes felt about her death. That brought another wave of guilt down on him, like a load emptied from a dump truck.

"My late wife could be a very difficult person at times." He searched for the right words to explain Eve. "She placed a high value on material possessions and community status. It sounds cliché, but love blinded me to who she truly was. In the early days of our marriage, I was just starting out as a CPA. By then, our relationship had become so fractious, I lost hope an explanation would make any difference."

"Must have been hard to give all that love with little in return."

Chalissa's quiet acknowledgment soothed a wound in his heart he hadn't paid attention to. He had suffered from Eve's withdrawal from their relationship. "There was one Valentine's Day when I thought things might get better. I surprised her with a diamond pendant I had scrimped and saved for months. Her attitude changed and she started to show more affection, but then I realized our relationship would only hum along nicely if I gave her similar baubles on a regular basis."

For a moment, neither one of them spoke. Titus hoped he hadn't overshared too much. Time to change the subject. "How'd you enjoy reading the book to Sam?"

Chalissa smiled, the gesture chasing the last of the shadows from her face. "It's a fun story. Sam is clearly all-in. He tried to bribe me to read a second chapter, and I admit I was tempted to find out what happens to Hugo."

Titus smiled back. "He's always angling for more story time."

"I enjoyed dinner."

"Me too." He stared into her eyes, not wanting the evening to end. "Want some coffee?"

"I shouldn't. It's getting late. I should go." But she didn't move.

"You probably should." He waited for her to make a move but her gaze remained tangled with his. Without thinking of the consequences, he gave into temptation and traced his finger along her jawline.

Chalissa angled her head slightly to the right and moved a half step closer to him. They stood with their bodies nearly touching, her hand resting on his arm and his fingers lightly caressing her cheek.

Titus ignored his brain warning at how bad an idea this was in favor of dropping his gaze to her lips. He leaned down slowly, giving her plenty of time to step back. His lips brushed hers, but before he could deepen the kiss, Chalissa pulled out of his arms as if yanked by an invisible hook.

Avoiding his gaze, she ducked her head. Her cell phone rang and she fumbled in her back jeans pocket for her phone. "I'm sorry, but I need to take this call." Turning away, she answered it. "Hello."

Her breathless tone pleased him. Maybe she'd been as affected by the quick kiss as he'd been. Deep, even breaths slowed his racing heart and crossing his arms kept his hands from reaching for her again. Would she have allowed him to deepen the kiss if a call hadn't distracted them both?

He couldn't make out her murmured conversation, but the tensing of her shoulders doused his emotions with cold water. Something wasn't right.

Ending the call, she turned back to him. "That was Mac. Federal prosecutor Leela Burgess has been in a car accident."

Titus sucked in a breath. The woman who believed the video evidence against him? "Is she okay?"

Chalissa shook her head. "No, she's dead."

# CHAPTER 16

"**D**ead?" Titus had heard Chalissa correctly, but his brain wasn't processing that the lead federal prosecutor on his case had died in a vehicle accident.

"She was pronounced dead at the scene." Chalissa typed what Titus assumed was a text. "I'm letting the inspectors outside know what happened."

He waited until she finished. "What happened?"

"The sheriff's office is still investigating the cause, but the officers on the scene said her car ran off the road and hit a tree."

"Where was the accident?" Surely this couldn't be a coincidence. It must be related to the warning sent to the courthouse.

She consulted her phone. "On Siloam Road, about thirty miles outside of Winston-Salem, North Carolina."

"Any witnesses?"

"Mac said a homeowner was waiting to turn out of his driveway onto Siloam Road when Ms. Burgess's car approached at a high speed. She appeared to lose control of the vehicle and her car left the road, smashing headfirst into a tree." She met his eyes. "It was raining lightly, so slippery road conditions might have contributed to the crash."

He swallowed hard. "Does Mac think this is tied to the trial?"

"He can't say for certain. But we'll continue to stick close to you and Sam just the same." She smothered a yawn behind one hand. "Sorry, I was at work by five thirty this morning to help process a new witness."

He should tell her to go home. But he didn't want her to leave. Not after receiving news of a possible death connected with his case. His wanting her to stay had everything to do with the case—and nothing to do with the aborted kiss. But the tired lines hugging her eyes changed his mind. "You should go home."

Her eyebrows raised at his adamant tone.

He held up a hand. "Not that I don't want you to stay. Wait a minute, that didn't come out right—too many negatives." He laughed, and her answering smile did funny things to his insides. "I want you to stay, but we've both had a long day."

"Is it still Monday?"

Her question made him smile. "Yeah, it is." Trailing her to the living room, he leaned against the mantel while she gathered her bag. "What are your plans for Saturday?"

"What I usually do—catch up on paperwork and go for a run. Why do you ask?"

"Oh, I almost forgot. The weather forecast cleared enough that Sam's Trail Life USA troop is going hiking on Saturday."

Chalissa shook her head. "I don't think that's a good idea."

"Sam wanted to invite you to come with us." Sam had asked if Chalissa could come, but it was Titus who was hoping she'd say yes for reasons that had nothing to do with her protecting him and his son. At her hesitation, he added, "The Marshals vetted the troop leadership and members when Sam joined in September, and we always stick together as a troop on these hikes. There will be lots of other adults to help keep an eye on Sam and the other boys."

"It's not the other troop members I'm worried about."

While he understood her priority was their safety, he refused to live—and let Sam live—in a bubble. To his mind, hiking with a group of trusted adults and boys was about as safe as staying in their house. "Sam's been looking forward to this. April's been so rainy, we had to scrap our campout a couple of weeks ago. Please. There's so much Sam can't or doesn't want to even try. Hiking is something he loves."

Her face softened. "Okay, we'll figure out how to make it work. And I have been wanting to explore some of the hiking trails around here. Where are you going?"

"The Billy Goat Trail. We're not doing the entire trail, but the section with the rock scramble."

"I'll bet Sam will love that." She smiled. "What time?"

Her acceptance of his invitation had his heart beating more rapidly. "We were planning on leaving by seven, if you want to ride with us."

"Sounds great." She moved to the door. "I'll drive over here to make things easier."

"Sounds great," he echoed her words, then grinned, happier than Sam over winning this past Friday night's rummy card game.

Her eyes sparkled. "Okay then. Bye."

Dazzled by the light in her brown eyes, he once again parroted her. "Bye."

She slipped out the door. As much as he wanted to watch her walk to her vehicle, he shut the door. If he wasn't mistaken, U.S. Marshal Chalissa Manning had been flirting with him, and the thought both pleased and terrified him.

Saturday morning dawned sunny. Chalissa breathed the crisp air. In the parking lot of Great Falls Visitor Center, she nodded to the two Marshals, who'd dressed for hiking but would keep an eye on the comings and goings of the hikers. Another pair of Marshals patrolled the trail's other parking lot.

Chalissa laced her hiking boots, tucking in the ends as she'd done so many times for Brandon. If she didn't secure the loops and ends of the laces, he would inevitably trip over them. His clumsiness had annoyed everyone but her. To Chalissa, it was just part of who Brandon was. Even all these years after his death, she winced at the memories of other kids making fun of his walking into desks, doors, and walls. Of his tripping up and down stairs. Of the hurt in his eyes when an adult laughed too. Some teachers had even made cutting remarks like, "If he didn't want to be made fun of, he should be more careful." As if simply telling Brandon to stop being clumsy would actually help him not to be so inept.

"Ready, Miss Chalissa?"

At Sam's eager question, Chalissa shoved away the memories of the past and straightened, slinging her small daypack over her shoulders. "Ready, Sam."

He grabbed her hand. "Let's go!"

With a laugh, she allowed Sam to pull her over to a group of a dozen or so boys, accompanied by their dads. Titus had introduced her to the adults when they'd arrived ten minutes ago. She was the only female in the group, but while the other dads threw her curious looks, no one commented on her presence with the Davis family.

"This is Miss Chalissa," Sam announced to the boys, who ranged in age from six to fourteen, from what Titus had told her on the drive to the parking lot. "She's going out with my dad."

Chalissa blinked at the introduction, but managed a smile as Sam rattled off the names of the boys. When he'd finished, she gave the group a general, "Nice to meet you," before easing away to stand by Titus while the leaders organized the boys into smaller groups for the hike.

"Well, that was awkward," she said.

"True, but awkward," he agreed, his brown eyes twinkling. "Sam is nothing if not forthright."

"I'll have to remember that."

"Titus, you, Sam, and Chalissa will be in the rear group with Taylor and Jamal and Leon and Sean," Troop Master Denny Brown said. "We'll do section A, which includes the rock scramble, and then return to the parking lot. Should take about ninety minutes or so."

"Sounds good. Sam?" Titus called to his son, who immediately trotted over. "We're with Taylor and Leon, today."

Sam's face fell. "Okay."

Titus didn't seem to notice his son's demeanor. "I'll go check in with their dads."

"Okay." Chalissa put her hand on Sam's shoulder. "Don't you like Taylor and Leon?"

Head down, Sam toed the gravel with his hiking boot. "They don't like me."

"Why not?"

"Because."

Chalissa probed gently. "Because why?"

Sam blew out a breath, raising his head. The tears shimmering in his eyes made her heart ache, but she kept her expression interested rather than let compassion color her expression.

"Because they never talk to me." He kicked a rock hard, sending it several feet away. "At the meetings, they only talk to each other."

"Do you talk to them?"

Sam stopped kicking gravel. "I've tried."

"How?" Chalissa saw the first group of boys and dads head up the trail.

"I say hi to them, but they never say anything but hi back."

"Maybe you should try something else." She placed a hand on his shoulder as the second group hit the trail.

"Sam, Chalissa, time to go." Titus waved them over to where he stood with Jamal and Sean, their sons beside them.

"Like what?" Sam fell into step beside her as they approached Titus.

"I've always found asking questions to be a good way to start a conversation," she said. "Think about what you like to do, and you could ask them if they like to do the same thing."

"I really like Pokémon," Sam said. "I could ask them if they play Pokémon."

"That would be a good start."

"Thanks, Miss Chalissa." Sam darted off to catch up with Leon and Taylor, who had started up the path ahead of their fathers.

Titus dropped back to walk beside her as they began the climb. "Whatever you did to get Sam to walk with the boys instead of us, thanks. I didn't think he'd leave my side once he saw who was in our group."

Chalissa shrugged. "I just suggested a way for him to connect with the other boys." She craned her neck to see Sam, who appeared to be in animated conversation with them. "He seems to be having a good time."

He held back a branch to allow her to pass before replying. "I worry about him." Titus dropped his voice. "Because of the autism, he has a hard time socially, and while he loves being outdoors and stuff, at the regular meetings, I often find him off by himself."

"It must be tough to see that." Her chest tightened. Brandon nearly always hung around the periphery of a group of kids, never quite belonging. When he did venture into the circle, usually whatever he tried to contribute to the conversation backfired, and the kids would push him out again. It broke her heart to see his struggles to fit in. But Sam wasn't Brandon. Things were different now. People knew more about autism and how to help kids overcome some of the social deficiencies from a young age.

"It is," he agreed.

Ahead, the boys scrambled up and over a boulder. Chalissa smiled at the sight of the joy on their faces. The late April weather had given them a picture perfect day—no clouds marred the bright blue sky as the sun shone down. The Potomac River sparkled down below the path, which hugged the cliffs alongside the water.

Soon, the trail took all of her concentration, and conversation dropped off between her and Titus. Rounding a corner, she gaped at the rock face reaching for the sky where a half dozen people climbed.

The troop had gathered at the base for a brief rest before tackling the summit.

"How are you doing?" Titus took a long drink from his water bottle, his T-shirt damp against his lower back.

"I didn't realize how many rocks we had to climb." She drank some water, wiping her mouth with the back of her hand. "And according to the trail map, we're not even halfway done."

"Not wimping out on me, are you?"

She shot him a grin. "Not a chance. I'm ready when you are."

The troop leader paired up boys and adults. Somehow, Sam got separated from Titus and Chalissa, who ended up with Taylor and Leon. Sam was in the first group to climb, the excitement on his face warring with her concern over the separation.

Waiting at the base for their turn to climb, Titus shielded his eyes from the sun. "Do you think he'll be okay without me?"

She replaced her water bottle in her pack. "Relax, Dad. He'll be fine."

"That obvious, huh?" he said.

"Yep." She checked that both boys had their laces tied tightly, then motioned for Taylor to start the climb. "I'll follow Taylor, then you send Leon up after me."

"Who put you in charge?" Titus joshed.

"During college, I spent a summer with A Christian Ministry in the National Parks and hiked a good portion of the Appalachian Trail." She gained a foothold and pulled herself up. "I know hiking."

"Oh, I'm not complaining. I rather like the view from down here."

Chalissa made a face at him under her arm, then turned her full attention to the climb. Twenty minutes later, she crested the summit and watched Titus maneuver the rest of the way up to join her. "You made it."

"Don't sound so surprised." Titus elbowed her in the ribs gently, his eyes alight with laughter. "I've done my share of hiking too." Uncapping his water bottle, he glanced around. "Do you see Sam?"

She did her own sweep of the area, where their group mingled with a large crowd of teenagers coming from the opposite direction to make their way down the rock face. "No, I don't see him yet."

Titus asked the two men who had been with Sam, but when they shook their heads, Chalissa could see the panic building in his eyes.

"Easy," she said in an undertone. "Remember, he's probably just down the trail a bit."

Titus nodded, but the worry didn't leave his eyes. "I know, but—"

"Mr. Davis! Mr. Davis!" Taylor rushed up, his face pale, Leon right behind him.

"What's wrong?" Titus gripped Taylor's shoulders. "Where's Sam?"

"He fell off the rock," Taylor gasped.

# CHAPTER 17

"W here?" Titus barely stopped himself from shaking Taylor. Fear poured over him like hot asphalt. He could barely hear the reply for the roaring in his ears.

"We were playing on the rocks right there," Taylor pointed to an outcropping barely visible from where they stood. "Some older kids were horsing around there, so we moved to the farthest boulder." He raised anxious eyes to Jamal, who had joined them. "We tried to stay safe."

Titus had heard enough. He took off for the rocks indicated where five boulders bunched together. A man lay on his stomach close to the edge of the farthest boulder, his attention on something out of Titus's line of sight.

Titus scrambled over the rocks to the man.

The man raised himself up on his elbows, turning his head to look at Titus. "Hi. I'm Evan. Are you Sam's dad?"

"Yes." Titus swallowed hard and crouched down. "How is he?"

"Thank goodness, he landed on a short ledge. He's conscious, but I think his arm is hurt." Evan got to his knees to make room for Titus. "See for yourself."

Titus dropped to his belly near the edge and peered over to see the top of Sam's head. "Hey, buddy, how are you?"

"Dad?"

The fear and relief in Sam's voice brought tears to his eyes. "I'm here. How are you doing?"

"I fell." Sam swiped at his nose with his left arm, while keeping his right close to his body. "I hurt my arm."

"Okay, don't move. We'll get you out." Titus rose to his knees.

"Is he okay?" Chalissa knelt beside Titus.

"He's on a small ledge with a hurt arm." Relief that Sam was all right vied with growing concern about his precarious position—and that his son wouldn't panic and fall off the ledge.

She leaned over Titus's shoulder. "Sam, hang in there. Help is on the way."

Titus eyed the distance between where he sat and Sam's location. Probably not more than fifty feet, but the rock formation complicated things. Sam rested on a small ledge, leaving very little room for anyone to occupy the space beside him. "Maybe I can rappel down to him." Although, how he'd do that, Titus had no idea. But to save his son, he was willing to try.

"Not possible," another man said. He held up a hand as Titus started to argue. "I'm an experienced climber, and even I couldn't stand on that ledge. I'm too big."

"He's being modest," the third man said. "This is Yancy, who owns Great Falls Rock Climbing, just down the road, and I'm Ryan."

Titus vaguely recalled driving by the business right before turning into the parking lot.

"Chalissa gave us a call to see if we could help," Yancy said.

"I also called 911," Chalissa interjected. "ETA is thirty to forty minutes away."

Titus groaned in frustration. He rolled onto his stomach again and leaned as far over the edge as he dared. "I'm here, Sam. Help is coming."

"I'm scared. I want to go home." Sam pushed his glasses up on his nose, leaving a smear of dirt across his face. "Can't you come get me now?"

"I wish I could, but the ledge is too small for both of us to fit on it." Titus tried to keep the panic from his own voice. "But don't worry—I'll wait up here with you the entire time. It won't seem that long."

"Okay," Sam sniffed.

Titus racked his brain with something to take Sam's mind off the pain of his arm. "Knock, knock."

Sam's head lifted, his eyes bright with tears. "Who's there?"

"Goliath," Titus said.

"Goliath who?" Sam replied.

"Goliath down, you looketh tired," Titus finished the joke.

A smile fought its way through Sam's tears. "Tell me another one, Dad."

"Knock, knock," Titus said. For the next few minutes, he told his son every knock-knock joke he could remember. Sam giggled a little at the silliness, but the trepidation never left his eyes.

"Titus?"

Titus twisted around to see Chalissa adjusting a buckle on a harness. "What are you doing?"

She tugged on one of the straps. "Getting ready to rescue Sam."

Her matter-of-fact tone should have soothed him, but all he could think of was her plummeting to her death trying to help his son. "You can't. You'll fall. I can't lose—" He bit off the words before he could blurt out "you too." How had she become more than someone protecting him and Sam? He couldn't think about that now—not with Sam hurt.

"I'll be fine. I've done this a time or two." She patted his shoulder, then moved to talk to Ryan while Yancy secured one end of a purple nylon rope around a sturdy tree next to the boulder.

"But the ledge is small. It won't fit both of you." Titus pitched his voice low so Sam wouldn't overhear his concerns.

"Yancy thinks there will be just enough room for me to stand beside Sam," Chalissa rejoined. She leaned closer to Titus, her brown eyes never leaving his. "I've had training in rappel rescues. I can do this safely for both me and Sam. Besides, Sam knows me, and we both know how unpredictable kids with autism can be when they're afraid."

"You'll have a better chance of getting him to follow instructions than a stranger," Titus said.

"It will be okay." She laid a hand on Titus's shoulder, then turned to accept a pair of gloves from Ryan. She slipped them on while he snapped the purple rope through a carabiner attached to her harness. "We all set?"

With a yank on her harness, Ryan gave her a thumbs up. "Yancy will belay you."

She nodded, then walked to the edge of the boulder and dropped the end of the rope over the side. "Sam? I'm going to come down and get you. I need you to stand up and press your back against the rock. Can you do that?"

Titus held his breath. Would Sam be able to follow her instructions? One misstep and his son would tumble over the edge. *Please God, help Sam.* He watched his son struggle to his feet, his left hand cradling his right arm, and move back as instructed. *Thank you, Lord.*

"Good job. Now stand real still and I'll be down in a jiffy." Chalissa turned around, her hands gripping the rope and her back to the edge of the rock. "Ready, Yancy?"

"Ready." Yancy steadied his stance, the rope looped around his waist, gloves on his hands as well.

With a jaunty wave of her hand, Chalissa gave a little hop and disappeared over the edge.

"HOW'RE YOU DOING, SAM?" CHALISSA CALLED AS SHE CLEARED THE edge. She smacked her knee into the rock before getting her feet underneath her. Definitely should have taken a refresher course last year when she'd had the opportunity. The concaveness of the rock made finding purchase for rappelling difficult, but after the first misstep, she found her feet.

"Okay, Miss Chalissa."

The thready tone to his voice made her move a little faster. With her feet against the rock's surface, she walked her way down to the ledge. Balancing on the rock, she assessed the space between Sam and the sheer drop down into the trees. Up close, there was less room than anticipated. But she'd make it work. "I'm going to come to you now. Hold steady."

Without waiting for his affirmation, she moved to the right, walking her feet sideways on the rock. Touching down lightly on the ledge rim, she gave the rope a single tug to indicate she'd reached the ledge. "Hey, Sam. Ready to get out of here?"

"Yes." He cradled his right arm close to his body. "I hurt my arm."

"I know. We'll try not to jostle you on the way up." Chalissa softened her voice. "In fact, I think my magic helpers are sending me something right now." She snapped her fingers and a rope dropped from above, a bundle hooked to it by a carabiner.

"Wow. How'd you do that?" Sam's eyes widened.

She pulled the rope toward her and released the bundle. "I told you—magic helpers." She smiled briefly at the puzzled expression on his face. Unwrapping the bundle, she held out a modified harness. "I think this will fit you. Let's get you suited up and back up top."

Working quickly, she coaxed Sam into the harness, then wrapped his injured arm in an ace bandage before putting it in a jerry-rigged sling from Titus's flannel shirt. "Now for the hard part."

Sam swallowed, tears trickling down his face. "My arm really hurts."

"I know, but can you be brave for a few more minutes?"

"I think so."

"Good." She positioned herself in front of him. "I've created a foot loop for you to stand in. I'm also going to clip you to the lead rope, so you can't fall. Got it?"

He nodded, his eyes darting from the rope to her face.

Moving quickly, she used locking carabiners to secure him to the rope, then talked him through putting his left foot into the loop. "Hold on to me here," she indicated a loop on her shoulder harness, "with your left hand. You'll swing a little, but not far from me at all."

Chalissa waited until he'd complied with her instructions, then tugged the rope again. "I'm going to start climbing back up."

"Wait! I'm not ready!" Sam clawed at her.

She caught his hand with hers. "Sam, look at me." When he did, she leaned her forehead against his. "I've done this many times. The man helping me has done this many times. We will be okay. Your dad is waiting at the top. You can do this. You're a brave boy."

He bit his lip. "Will you pray for me? Dad says Jesus helps us when we're scared."

The simple request tightened her chest. Would God hear a prayer from her when they hadn't spoken for so long? But another glance into Sam's terrified eyes had her nodding. "Sure."

He closed his eyes, the trust making her throat clog for a moment. She could do this. Titus prayed as if talking to a friend. Piece of cake, right?

Clearing her throat, she said softly, "Dear God, please help Sam be brave and keep us both safe as we climb up. Amen."

Sam opened his eyes. "Thanks, Miss Chalissa. I'm ready now."

After securing Sam, she tugged the rope again, then moved to the left off the ledge, her feet connecting with the rock's surface. Sam dangled to her right. By extending her legs, she kept his body away from the rock as she walked up the rock. The short distance felt like an eternity with the extra weight of Sam along with her own body.

When they crested the top, Titus helped Sam over the top, while Ryan gave her an assist. Standing firmly on the rock, Ryan unclipped the boy, who tumbled into his father's arms, sobbing. Chalissa panted from the exertion, one thought looping in her mind. Had Sam fallen—or had he been pushed?

# CHAPTER 18

Titus paced outside the imaging room while Sam got his arm x-rayed behind the closed door. His mind raced with possibilities about how the morning's mishap had happened. Top of his mind was the fear someone had deliberately pushed Sam over the edge. During the ambulance ride to the hospital, he couldn't shake the feeling something about the fall wasn't accidental. Chalissa, who had driven his car to the hospital behind the ambulance, leaned against the wall, her head ducked as she texted on her phone.

When she slipped her phone back into her pocket, he asked, "Any news?"

Before she could reply, the technician wheeled Sam out of the room. "His arm is definitely broken," the tech said, pausing to allow an orderly pushing a woman in a wheelchair to pass. "We'll take him back to the Emergency Department and get him fitted with a temporary splint to allow the swelling to go down. Then you'll need to go to a children's orthopedic doctor for casting."

"My arm really hurts, Dad." Sam sniffled, his cheeks wet with tear tracks.

"I know." Titus walked alongside the gurney as the tech headed down the hall. "We'll get you some pain medicine when we get back to the emergency room."

Titus told a few more knock-knock jokes on the way back to the ED cubby Sam had been assigned to. The tech left just as a nurse bustled in.

"Sam, I'm Mike, your nurse." The male nurse hooked up the blood pressure cuff, then showed Sam a chart of pain faces. "Tell me which face you feel like right now."

Sam pointed to one indicating a pain level of eight.

"Your arm must hurt a lot." Mike made a notation in the computer. "Can you swallow pills?"

"Yeah." Sam wilted against the pillows and Titus smoothed back a lock of his hair. His son's face had very little color against the white sheets.

"That true, Dad?" Mike asked.

"Yes, if they're no bigger than an Extra Strength Tylenol capsule."

"I'll be right back." Mike left.

"Hey, Sam." Chalissa moved up to the head of the bed. "You doing okay?"

The boy nodded.

"Can you tell me what happened on the rocks?"

Sam's lower lip trembled. "I slipped and fell."

Mike came back in holding a paper cup. "Here you go. Two ibuprofen pills. These will help with the pain." The nurse helped Sam with the pills and water. "I'll be back in a little bit with the temporary splint."

Chalissa walked Sam through the accident. Titus listened intently, not interrupting her gentle questioning. Something about the way Sam talked about it made Titus think his son wasn't telling the entire truth. Mike entered with the implements for the splint. Chalissa stepped over to Titus while the nurse eased the splint onto Sam's arm.

"What do you think?" He pitched his voice low to keep Sam from overhearing.

"Police questioned both boys. Taylor said that he didn't see Sam fall at all, only heard him yell." Chalissa pulled out her phone and tapped the screen. "But Leon said a man had spoken to Sam before he and Taylor jumped to the farthest rock."

Titus reminded himself to breathe, as confirmation of his fears accelerated his heart rate. "What did this man say?"

"Leon didn't hear, but he said Sam talked to the man for a few minutes before joining the boys on the other rock."

"Was Leon able to describe the man?"

"Yes." Chalissa held out her phone to Titus. On the screen, a color sketch of a stranger stared back. "The police used a composite app to put together a sketch of the man. This isn't as good as working with an artist, but it does have the advantage of capturing his impressions immediately. Do you recognize him?"

Titus accepted the phone and took a closer look. The man wore a Washington Nationals baseball cap pulled low over his eyes, shadowing his face. Brown eyes, dark brown hair, a close-cropped beard. Nothing looked familiar. "Sorry, I don't think I've ever seen him before."

"Maybe Sam can shed some light on his identity." She took her phone back.

"Did anyone else see this man?"

"A few teenagers saw the man talking to Sam, but their description matches Leon's. The teens were too far away to hear any conversation between Sam and this man."

"So we have no way of knowing if this man had anything to do with Sam's fall or if it was just a coincidence that he spoke to Sam prior to the accident." The uncertainty of whether his son had been targeted to send a message to him about testifying ratcheted up the tension.

"No, but Evan, the man who stayed with Sam after he fell, said he —that is, Evan—called out to Sam to be careful right before Sam fell."

Titus stilled as he absorbed the new information. "Evan saw Sam fall?"

"Yes," she said. "The police checked out his story. Another hiker backed him up, said he'd also noticed Sam stood too close to the edge."

"I should have kept a closer eye on him." But he hadn't. Instead, he'd chosen to enjoy Chalissa's company. Secretly wishing they were really dating, and not just pretending as a cover.

"It looks like something startled him and he slipped over the edge."

"Truly an accident." He watched the nurse ease the strap of the sling around Sam's shoulders. "I suppose that's good news."

"No one saw where the man in the baseball cap went."

"Maybe he'd already left the area before Sam's fall."

"That's possible."

Mike finished adjusting the sling's strap. "Okay, we're all set. I'll be back with the paperwork so you can get this young man home. I told him to remember to take it easy until he gets the cast on."

"Thank you." Titus moved to the bed and ruffled Sam's hair. "Feeling any better?"

"I think so." Sam yawned. "Can I watch an episode of The Last Airbender on your phone?"

"Sure." He opened the streaming app and engaged the parental controls before handing the phone to Sam. "Keep the volume low, okay?"

Sam nodded, his fingers already busy swiping to find the show.

Chalissa beckoned him closer. "When Sam's feeling better, we need to ask him if the man he saw today was the same one outside his bedroom window."

# CHAPTER 19

Titus hadn't thought about the possibility of a connection between the man outside Sam's window and the man on the rocks. "You think it's the same man?" Sam's description of the man wearing a Nationals baseball cap played in his mind. "Because of the baseball hat?"

"It's a lead we're following." She held up a hand. "I know there are a lot of Nationals fans around here, but I don't like coincidences."

Sam appeared engrossed in the show, but Titus angled closer to Chalissa just in case his son was trying to eavesdrop. "If this was connected to the trial, what's the purpose? It doesn't appear that the man pushed Sam."

"We're looking into every possibility."

"I wanna go home now." Sam let the phone drop to the bed.

Titus hustled to the bed. "We'll go as soon as we get the discharge papers."

His son's lower lip trembled. "I don't wanna wait."

Chalissa joined him on the side of the bed. "I know your arm hurts a lot, but it will start to feel better tomorrow. Soon, you'll get a cast. Then it will only ache a bit."

"Really?" Sam fashioned his gaze on her face.

She tilted her head. "I guess you could say I'm an expert." She leaned closer to Sam. "I broke my arm twice when I was a kid."

"The same one?" Sam's eyes widened.

"Nope." Chalissa kept her attention on his son. "I broke this arm," she pointed to her right arm, "when I was five. The left when I was six." A shadow crossed her face. "My older brother had even more broken bones. One of his legs," she ticked them off on her fingers, "his collarbone, and three of his fingers—at the same time."

"Wow, that's a lot of broken bones." The awe in Sam's voice didn't mirror the concern building in Titus's chest. "How did you break your arm?

"Nothing as exciting as what happened to you."

As Sam questioned Chalissa about how she handled wearing a cast, Titus puzzled over Chalissa's story about broken bones. Sure, some kids were more prone to break bones than others—he had suffered from a broken nose and a broken wrist from a skateboarding accident in middle school. But something about the way she spoke of hers and her brother's injuries hinted at their origins not in normal kid-related activities.

When Sam wound down his questions, Chalissa held out her phone, the drawing of the man in the ball cap on the screen. "Is this the man who talked to you before you fell?"

Sam wrinkled his nose, his eyes narrowing as he examined the picture. "Yeah, that's him." He looked up at Chalissa, then at his father, confusion clouding his gaze. "How did you get such a good picture of him?"

"Taylor and Leon saw him talking to you and gave the police a description." Chalissa paused, exchanging a glance with Titus. They had discussed whether to ask Sam if the man on the rocks was the same face he saw outside his window. Now he nodded for her to go ahead and ask Sam. "Is he the same man who you saw outside your window?"

Sam flicked his eyes back toward the phone. "Maybe, I think so." Tears flooded his eyes. "I don't know." The last words came out in a wail.

"Hey, it's okay." Chalissa laid the back of her hand on his flushed cheek. Sam leaned into her hand. "If you're not sure, you're not sure. No big deal."

The gesture reminded Titus sharply of how much Sam missed not having a mother. Eve hadn't been tender in her ministrations to Sam, but that might have been because he had been a fussy baby, screaming from colic most evenings until he reached four months old. Eve hadn't handled those nights well. Even all these years later, his ears still rang with the things she'd yelled at him over Sam's cries. Some days, he came close to thanking God she hadn't lived to say the same things to Sam when he could understand her.

Sam scrubbed at his face with his left hand. "I can't be sure. It was dark."

She put her phone away. "What did the man on the rocks say to you?"

"He, uh, asked me if I liked birds." Sam turned to his father. "He wasn't asking me to leave with him or personal information. I told him that I did like birds."

"That's fine," Titus reassured his son. "What did the man say next?"

"He said farther up the trail, there was a lookout point where you could see the nest of a red-tailed hawk." Sam's eyes lit up. "He told me how to find it when we got to that part of the trail."

"We'll have to look for it the next time we hike Billy Goat," Titus promised.

"The boys said you went rather quickly over the farthest rock," Chalissa said. "Why was that?"

"The man pointed out a Downy Woodpecker drilling a tree over there. I wanted to see it before the bird flew away." Sam dropped his gaze to the bed. "I forgot the rules about being careful on the rocks. I tripped. That's why I fell." Tears squeezed out of Sam's eyes.

Titus sat down on the bed, careful not to jostle Sam's injured arm. "We all make mistakes. I'm glad you're okay."

A man wearing a white lab coat came into the room, introducing himself as Dr. Bayer.

"The break is a non-displaced fracture, which means that the bones didn't separate when breaking," Dr. Bayer said.

"When will he get a cast?" Titus asked.

"I think by Tuesday, any swelling will have subsided enough. I recommend you see a children's orthopedic surgeon for the cast." The doctor smiled at Sam. "And no running or jumping until you have a cast—you don't want to hurt that arm any further."

The nurse came back in with a sheaf of papers in his hand. "Here are the discharge papers and instructions on how to care for the arm until you see the orthopedic surgeon."

"Thank you." Titus folded the papers and tucked them under his arm. "Ready to go home, Sam?"

"Uh-huh." Sam slid off the bed as the doctor and nurse said their goodbyes.

As Chalissa drove them home in his SUV, Titus puzzled over the composite of the man in the Nationals cap. While he didn't recognize the man, something about him was familiar. But he couldn't dredge up the connection his brain was trying to make. He'd let it go for now, hoping his subconscious would do the work for him if left alone. For now, he sent up a prayer of thanksgiving for Sam's rescue—along with a prayer for strength to resist the allure of the very attractive U.S. Marshal beside him.

CHALISSA STUFFED THE TAKEOUT CONTAINER INTO THE TRASH CAN, then washed her hands at the kitchen sink. After an early dinner, since they had skipped lunch, she tackled the cleanup while Titus settled Sam into bed to listen to a disc from his Story of the World CD collection. While she longed to relax in a hot bubble bath, she needed to update Titus on the new information the Marshals had received relating to his upcoming trial.

"Want some decaf coffee?" Titus looked as tired as she felt.

"Sure." She wrung out the sponge and moved away from the sink so he could access the Keurig.

"I suspect he'll be out like a light before the CD ends," he said. "Even though it's only six thirty."

She smothered a yawn behind her hand. "He's not the only one."

"Maybe we should do this another time."

"No, the coffee will perk me up." Another yawn belied her words. "There are some things we need to discuss."

"Sounds ominous."

"I don't think *ominous* would apply. However, if you don't mind, I'll wait until I have some coffee first before explaining."

He nodded his agreement. While the coffee brewed, they shared a companionable silence. Handing her a thick mug, he gestured toward the backyard. "Want to sit on the deck? Might be a little chilly, but I keep several blankets out there."

"Perfect." She followed him through the sliding glass door and out on the wooden deck. She picked a chaise lounge, putting her mug on a glass-topped wrought iron side table.

"Here you go." He tossed her a soft blue blanket, then tucked an army green one around him.

"Thanks." The blanket was the perfect weight to ward off the spring chill as the sun streaked the sky with orange, red, and yellow. A bird trilled its song, answered by a feathered friend. Azalea bushes lined one corner of the yard, their bright burst of color attesting to the warm Virginia spring. Breathing in deeply, she caught the whiff of charcoal riding on the back of freshly cut grass. The chaos of the day began to drain away. "This is lovely."

"Yes, it is."

She looked at Titus, who was studying her, not the landscape. The intensity of his gaze brought heat to her cheeks. While she longed for this to be a normal relationship, one where she could accept compliments and return them, she had to keep things professional. Or at least try very hard to not let herself get caught up in their pretend relationship. "Titus—"

"I know." He cut her off with a smile tinged with sadness. "I've been a widower for nearly seven years. In all that time, I haven't met anyone like you."

Picking up her coffee, she sipped to give her mouth something to do—otherwise, she might say something that would cross the line between witness and Marshal.

"I know you agreed pretend dating would be a good cover for Sam's sake, and it is. He doesn't suspect anything out of the ordinary. But I can't keep acting like I'm pretending to like you when I do." Shoving his hand into his hair, he sighed. "It's been a long time since I've been attracted to another woman. I want to know—before we go back to pretending—if things were different..."

She drew in a deep breath as he left the rest of his thought unsaid. "You mean if I wasn't a Marshal and you my witness, would there be a chance for an *us*?"

"Yes."

His simple answer along with the longing in his eyes nearly undid her resolve. It was madness to even consider answering him truthfully, and yet the words tumbled out despite her conviction it would likely ignite the attraction between them. "Then yes."

The words floated on the air between them, the knowledge drawing them closer together even though neither of them moved a muscle. For several minutes, Chalissa allowed herself to dream of a future with Titus and Sam. Of being intertwined in their lives. To finally have a family of her own.

Then, as if someone had snipped an invisible thread, the spell was broken. She blinked as if awakening from a dream, took another sip of her now-tepid coffee, and pulled out her phone to key up her notes. "There's still nothing new about Ms. Burgess's accident, although the sheriff's office has concurred it does look suspicious."

Good, her voice sounded firm, not shaky like her insides. For a second, the thought of Titus kissing her had nearly broken her resolve. She cleared her throat. "We'll know more early next week after the FBI lab has a chance to go over the car thoroughly. But we do know Burgess was coming from Janet Devonshire's home. One of Janet's nieces had called to say she'd found another cell phone registered to Janet."

"Wait, what?" His brow furrowed. "I thought the prosecutors said the estate had given them Janet's phone to prove the video came directly from her device."

"That's what they said." She consulted her notes. "Now there's a question as to whether the device was really Janet's phone or a clone."

The hope blooming in Titus's eyes made her feel like a heel for bursting the bubble, but she poked it with a pin anyway. "However, the prosecutor's office was very clear they are not ready to discount the video evidence and are continuing to probe into your financials."

"I feel like there's two steps forward, then one giant step back in all of this." He shrugged, frustration apparent in the tightening of his lips. "The trial starts a week from Monday, and we still don't know who's behind the video plant. Is the video connected with the threat delivered to the courthouse? Then there's this man in a Nationals baseball cap who may or may not be stalking my son. Are the two things related or is this stuff with Sam a very weird coincidence?"

"I don't know, but we're trying our best to find out." The pain in his voice drove her to cross to his chaise and sit on the end by his feet. She touched the back of his hand, and he turned his over to hold on tightly. "But I promise I won't rest until we discover who's behind this —and you and Sam are safe."

He squeezed her hand. "Thank you."

For a moment, neither one of them moved. The air hummed between them, playing a melody only the two of them heard. Slowly, as if moving through wet cement, Chalissa swayed toward Titus until their faces hovered within inches of each other. Her brain screamed at her to flee, but her body fused to the lounge.

"Chalissa." Titus breathed her name, the sound of it shimmering over her like a gentle breeze. His free hand tangled with the hair brushing the back of her neck, sending shivers all the way to her toes. "If you keep looking at me like that, I'm going to kiss you."

"How am I looking at you?" She needed to know, in case she ever wanted him to kiss her again. Which was just plain silly. She shouldn't want him to kiss her now, but her common sense had apparently taken a detour tonight, leaving her with a heart pushing her to see if his lips really felt as soft as they had during their aborted kiss.

He closed the gap until only a sliver of air hung between them. His breath brushed her lips, and she nearly gasped at the sensation. One of the azalea bushes rustled, distracting her. Narrowing her eyes to focus in the glooming of early evening, she pulled back slightly.

"Chalissa?"

"Shhh." She leaned closer to him as if mesmerized by his presence, placing her mouth near his ear. "I think someone or something's in the azalea bushes."

Titus reflexively started to turn his head, but she laid her hand on his cheek to stop him. The rough texture of his beard contrasted with the smoother skin of her palm. But now wasn't the time to revel in how wonderful it felt to caress his face. "Don't look. Act natural, like we don't notice anything amiss."

She pulled out her phone, turning on the camera's selfie function. "Smile." She angled her head close to his and snapped a photo, then she laughed as though he'd said something funny. Scrolling on her phone, she pulled up her texting and sent a message to the agent stationed on the street outside the house. "I let the Marshals sitting outside know we might have a situation here."

"Okay." He huddled close to her. "Should I check on Sam?"

"No, with Marshal Burlington guarding the front and us in the back with eyes on Sam's window, I think he's okay. Better to act like nothing's wrong and—"

The sliding glass doors behind them exploded outward, shards of glass raining down on them. Instinctively, Chalissa grabbed Titus by the shoulders and rolled him off the chaise lounge. Her head cracked against something hard and the world went dark.

# CHAPTER 20

S moke poured out of the house. Sam! Titus had to get to his son. Beside him, Chalissa lay on her side facing away from him. He nudged her shoulder but she didn't move. "Chalissa? I need to get Sam!"

Sirens wailed in the distance. Titus shook Chalissa hard. He had to get to Sam but he couldn't leave her lying on the deck.

"Mr. Davis?"

Titus glanced over his shoulder to spy a man dressed in jeans and a leather jacket crouching beside him.

The man flicked open a badge holder. "Marshal Palmer Glenn. You need to get away from the house now."

"I know, but my son's inside and Chalissa's not moving. I think she hit her head."

"Marshal Burlington went in through the front door to get Sam out. I'll help get Inspector Manning to safety." Glenn knelt beside Chalissa. "We have to get her away from the house. You grab her under the arms and I'll take her feet."

Smoke continued to roll out of the smashed sliding doors, propelling Titus to move. Together, he and the Marshal lifted and carried Chalissa off the deck and around the side to an oak tree at the far corner of the front yard, well away from the house. On the street, fire trucks roared to a halt. Gently placing her on the ground, he ran his hands lightly down the outline of her body without finding any obvious injuries.

His fingers then lightly probed the back of her head, but found no telltale bump. However, a stickiness on his fingers indicated a wound somewhere. The flashing lights provided enough light for him to see the gash on the side of Chalissa's head, blood mixing with her short hair. He pulled out a handkerchief and pressed it against the wound.

Her eyes fluttered. "Titus?"

"Dad!"

Titus turned to see a woman carrying Sam, presumably Marshal Burlington. She set Sam down and adjusted the strap on Sam's sling.

"I'll tend to Chalissa," the Marshal said.

Titus relinquished his hold on the handkerchief and concentrated on calming his son. "Sam, you okay?"

Sam hugged his hurt arm with his good one, then collapsed into his father's arms. "I'm scared. I was asleep, but then a loud noise woke me up."

Firemen raced around the opposite side of the house, hoses on their shoulders.

"Shhh, you're safe now." Titus tucked Sam into the crook of his arm.

Marshal Burlington spoke in low tones to Chalissa, who had propped herself up on her elbows in the grass.

"How's she doing?" Titus asked.

"She has a nasty cut on her head and might have a concussion," the other woman answered.

"I'm right here, you know." Chalissa struggled into a seated position. "I can hold the handkerchief myself. You go figure out what happened."

The Marshal gave Chalissa a long look, then scrambled to her feet and left.

"Miss Chalissa, you're bleeding." Sam twisted out of Titus's arms to kneel on the ground near Chalissa.

"Yeah, I got a wee cut on my head, but your dad gave me his hand-kerchief to stop the bleeding." She managed a smile but Titus caught a glimpse of the pain behind it.

"Good thing my dad always carries a handkerchief," Sam said. "Dad, my arm hurts a lot."

"I'm sure the EMTs will have something for you to take until we can get back in the house." What was taking the emergency respon-ders so long to come?

As if in answer to his unspoken query, two EMTs trotted up to them.

"What happened to your arm, young man?" A female emergency technician set down her bag, then dropped to her knees beside Sam, while her companion, a skinny man wearing a skull cap, began assessing Chalissa.

"I broke it earlier today, but I have to wait until Tuesday for the cast." Sam's eyes filled with tears. "It hurts."

"I bet it does. My name is Sam and I have something to help with the pain." The female EMT rummaged in her bag.

Titus gave up trying to pay attention to both Sam and Chalissa, focusing solely on EMT Sam.

"Your name is Sam? That's my name." Sam sniffed, momentarily distracted by the same name coincidence.

"Ah, but my name's short for Samantha. Is yours a nickname too?" She pulled out a syringe and a small bottle of medicine.

"No, it's just Sam."

"What pain medication did he have in the ED?" the EMT asked Titus.

"Only children's ibuprofen. We gave him another dose before he went to bed about," Titus consulted his watch, "an hour ago."

"Can you point to your pain level?" Samantha held up a pain chart. Sam touched the second to the last. "This one."

"So it hurts a whole lot?" Samantha put the chart back in her bag. His son nodded.

"Okay, I'm going to give you a shot of fentanyl in your leg. It will help you feel better." Samantha pushed up Sam's pajama pant leg.

"Dad," Sam grabbed Titus's hand, "I don't want a shot!"

"You can do it," Chalissa interjected. A white bandage hugged the left side of her hairline.

Sam sniffed, then nodded at the EMT, who promptly administered the shot. Sam winced, but didn't cry out—a marked improvement from the last time Titus had taken his son for a shot. It had taken Titus almost an hour to calm the sobbing child down. Granted, that had been a few years ago, but he had a feeling his son's stoic response now had more to do with Chalissa than Sam's growing maturity. The Marshal had connected with Sam in a way Titus hadn't thought possible, given how recently Chalissa had come into their lives.

"Ms. Manning, Mr. Davis, I'm Fire Marshal Roe. Could we have a word?" The fire marshal removed his helmet while the EMTs packed up their equipment.

"Ms. Manning, you should go to the hospital—I think the cut might need a couple of stitches," the male EMT said.

"I'll take care of it, I promise," Chalissa responded.

The EMT met Titus's gaze. "She really should see someone tonight."

Titus nodded. "I'll make sure she does."

Samantha paused before following her partner back to the ambulance. "The fentanyl will probably make him sleepy."

"Thanks." Titus looked from Chalissa to his son, who now stood barefoot in the grass. He should find out if they could return to the house—Sam looked done in.

Before the fire marshal could continue, Marshal Glenn walked up. "Hey, Sam. Let's go sit in my car while your dad talks to the fireman."

Titus ruffled Sam's hair. "Go with Mr. Glenn. I'll come get you in a few minutes."

Marshal Glenn slung an arm around Sam's shoulders. "Tell me how you got that fancy sling. Were you skydiving?"

"No, I was climbing on some rocks," Sam said.

Titus watched the pair until they reached the Marshal's SUV, then turned back to the fire marshal and Chalissa. "What happened?"

The fire marshal looked over his shoulder at the house, where firefighters walked back and forth along each side to the backyard, rolling hoses. "We were able to contain the fire, but one of my men smelled gas. Didn't leave a burner on by mistake, did you?"

Titus shook his head. "I didn't use the stove tonight at all."

"We turned off the gas to the house and have called the gas company, but until we know what happened, you can't stay in the house."

"Titus, I think I know of a *safe* place you and Sam can stay for a few days," Chalissa said before Titus could speak.

"That would be best," Roe said. "We'll know more in a few days after our inspector and the gas company takes a closer look."

Chalissa nodded. "Can Mr. Davis go inside now to gather some clothes and personal items?"

Roe shook his head. "We think all the gas has dissipated, but we don't want to run the risk of another build up." He handed a business card to Titus. "We'll be in touch."

As the fire marshal walked back to his men, Chalissa swayed slightly. Titus placed his hand under her elbow. She needed to go to the hospital and have that head wound properly taken care of. He cupped Chalissa's elbow more firmly. "Let's go."

"We need to strategize about where you're staying tonight first." She dug in her heels to resist his tugging, but Titus simply swept her up in his arms.

For a second, Chalissa said nothing, her brown eyes large and round. Giving her a jaunty smile, he strode toward the SUV where Marshal Glenn waited with Sam. He'd only taken a few steps when she stirred in his arms.

"Hey, I'm not an invalid," she hissed through clenched teeth as she kicked her legs. "Put me down."

He readjusted his grip, holding her squirming body closer to his.

Despite her wiggling, she filled his arms nicely. "Nope. You're going to the hospital. Now."

She growled something he didn't catch but stopped struggling. A few seconds later, they arrived at the SUV, and he reluctantly lowered her legs to the ground. The movement must have surprised her because she threw her arms around his neck.

"Easy there," he breathed as his hands fitted around her waist to steady her.

For a moment, she rested her forehead against his chest, her hands loosely clasped behind his neck. Gently, without any sudden moves, he lowered his cheek to rest against the right side of her head, luxuriating in the silkiness of her hair against his beard.

She stirred, raising her head but not stepping back. "Titus, I—"

"Where are Davis and Manning?" At the sound of Mac's voice, Chalissa sprang back, her shoulders smacking into the rear door of the SUV behind her.

Mac hurried up to them. "Are you two okay?"

"We're fine," Chalissa said.

"Chalissa has a nasty cut on her head that needs stitches," Titus contradicted her statement. "She needs to go to the hospital."

"How is Sam? I heard about the morning's accident." Mac looked from one to the other.

Titus ignored the second question in Mac's eyes about the tension between Chalissa and himself. Instead, he gave a brief update on Sam. "He's in the SUV with Mr. Glenn and probably asleep by now."

"Marshals Glenn and Burlington will take you and Sam to a safe house," Mac said.

Titus opened his mouth to protest, but Chalissa cut him off with an upraised hand.

"Your safety is our number-one priority. I'm only going to the hospital if you go with Glenn and Burlington to a safe house." She raised her eyebrows. "Are we clear?"

He leaned closer and whispered in her ear, "Yes, but you'd better keep your end of the bargain."

# CHAPTER 21

On Wednesday morning, the atmosphere at Spider Web Design pulsated with tension, as workers came back for the first day since the hostage situation. On his way to his cubicle, Titus counted at least twenty empty desks. Management had allowed employees to take the week off with pay and had provided counselors free of charge as well. While Sam's accident and the still-unexplained explosion in his house on Monday night had shaken him, the Marshals had reluctantly allowed him and Sam to stick to their normal routines. With Sam eager to show off his royal blue cast to his classmates, Titus had come to work.

Sipping his first cup of joe at his desk, he toyed with the idea of checking in with Chalissa. Except for a brief call last night, he had not spoken with her. He shouldn't have been so disappointed that she'd called instead of stopping by the safe house in person. But he was. Chalissa had gotten under his skin in a matter of days, and he couldn't get her off his mind. Even Sam appeared smitten, whining and fretting about her absence for most of yesterday.

"Titus, I need a word," Colby Matthews said, jolting Titus out of his thoughts.

"Sure, when?" Titus regarded his direct supervisor, the muscles in his stomach tightening. Seeing Matthews so soon after the merger announcement couldn't be good news.

The other man avoided Titus's gaze. His smartphone rang and he glanced at the screen. "I've got to take this, so come by my office in five minutes?"

"Okay," Titus said as Matthews left. Should he text Chalissa about the meeting? But tell her what, he had a bad feeling about it? No, he should concentrate on his work, not on a pretty Marshal he was only pretending to date. A quick check of his email revealed nothing that couldn't wait until after the meeting. Time to find out what Matthews wanted—and why his supervisor had looked so uncomfortable when talking with Titus.

Matthews's assistant smiled as Titus stopped by her desk. "You can go right in, Titus. He's expecting you."

"Thanks, Jewel." He subtly clenched and unclenched his hands to loosen the tension in his body, then gave the partially closed door a quick knock before pushing it open.

Matthews sat behind his desk, with the manager from Human Resources occupying one of the chairs in front of the desk.

Titus maintained his pleasant expression as he greeted both men, but the presence of Geoff Yates ratcheted up his concern. He couldn't afford to lose his position. He'd worked hard since entering WITSEC to rebuild his life, which included embarking on a new profession since anything to do with accounting—and his former life—was barred from him.

"Titus, I'm sure you realize that we've had to take a hard look at everyone as a result of this merger," Yates began, his gaze directed not at Titus but at the carpet.

Not a good sign at all. Titus clasped his hands together in his lap to keep from picking at his cuticles, a bad habit he engaged in when nervous.

"In your three years with Spider Web Design, you have done exemplary work," his supervisor added. "In fact, you're one of the top referrals here. Our clients regularly recommend you specifically to potential clients."

Titus straightened in his chair. The unexpected praise threw him, when he had been anticipating being let go. But the air in the room didn't lighten, leaving Titus to think there was more to come—and it wasn't good.

"Which is why this is so puzzling," Yates added, exchanging a look with Matthews.

When neither man continued for several seconds, Titus ventured a question, "What is puzzling?"

"You've been accused of sexual harassment," Matthews stated bluntly.

The accusation hit Titus like a load of cement. He stared at the man. "What?" He barely spoke to anyone at the office, much less the female employees. "I don't understand."

Yates opened a folder positioned on the corner of the desk. "Three weeks ago, Ms. Courtney Adams told a coworker your interactions with her made her uncomfortable."

"Courtney Adams?" Titus tried to place the name with a face, but came up blank. "I'm sorry, who is she?"

The HR manager raised his eyebrows, disbelief in every line of his face.

"She was the unit secretary for your department," Matthews replied in a tight voice.

The designation didn't help Titus's memory. "I'm sorry," he repeated, praying his tone conveyed not disinterest but genuine confusion. "I try to keep to myself at work, and I can't place her."

"Maybe this will help." Yates held out a piece of paper.

Titus accepted the paper, which had the head and shoulders photo of a young woman. The background suggested the photo had been snapped for the company ID badge. Blond hair framed a heart-shaped face. Blue eyes sparkled. A very pretty young woman, probably in her early twenties, Titus guessed. Much younger than his own thirty-six. Her face did jog his memory, and he recalled seeing her around the

145

office. "I think I've spoken to her maybe four or five times, but for no more than five minutes each time. Mostly I just said hello in passing."

Yates frowned, his head bent over the open folder on his lap. He fingered the top page. "Friday, Ms. Adams filed a formal sexual harassment claim against you."

"What did she say?" Maybe Titus had entered an alternative universe because nothing made sense anymore. First the video claiming he was in on the money laundering, then the workplace hostage situation, Sam's accident, and an explosion at his home. Now an accusation of sexual harassment at work. The timing seemed suspiciously coincidental—and unsettling, as if someone was out to not only discredit his testimony, but to destroy his life.

"That you sent her dozens of emails and texts in which you discussed your, er, desire for her," Yates said. "She brought copies of the emails and printouts of text screen shots."

Titus heard the words, but couldn't make sense of them. His head pounded like a jackhammer started drilling in his skull. "I've never emailed her or texted her either for work or outside of it. I don't understand why she's telling these lies."

"This isn't your email address?" Yates handed him one of the printed emails.

Titus couldn't stop his hand from shaking as he read his personal email address, td1494@gmail.com, on the from line. He'd created the address based on the year Luca Pacioli, the Italian recognized as the father of accounting and bookkeeping, published a book on the subject. The subject line of the email simply said, "Hey." But it was the content that sent the blood rushing to his face.

*When you walked into the office wearing that short skirt, I couldn't take my eyes off you. The way the fabric brushed against your thighs...*

Titus crumpled the paper, unable to read the rest. Shame filled him at the thought of Ms. Adams thinking he had actually sent an email like this. If the other emails had a similar theme, no wonder she'd filed suit.

"I didn't send this," he said quietly, raising his gaze to see both men looking at him, their expressions unreadable. "I would never send such an email to anyone, let alone a young woman I don't even know."

"She only brought a sample on Friday, but claims she has dozens of emails and texts that stretch back four weeks. That would mean the harassment started shortly after she joined the company," Yates said. "Per company policy, we've launched an investigation into these allegations."

Titus nodded. "I understand." And he did, but had no hope such an investigation would clear his name. Whoever had set him up had managed to hack into his personal email, and probably been able to spoof his phone number too. No one would believe his innocence, not with hard evidence like this to back up Ms. Adams's claims.

"I'll need that email back," Yates said.

Titus smoothed out the paper and started to hand it back when the date and time stamp at the top caught his eye. "Wait a minute." He studied the date more closely. "I couldn't have sent this email."

"What do you mean?" Matthews asked.

Titus pointed to the date. "It claims to have been sent on March 25 at eleven thirty at night, but my personal laptop was in the repair shop from March 24 to March 26."

"You could have sent it from your phone or other device," Yates pointed out.

"Then it would have said 'Sent from my iPhone,'" Titus replied. "Like all emails I send from my phone do. This email doesn't have that designation."

He looked from one man to the other, but only saw resolution on Yates's face and confusion on Matthews's. His supervisor wanted to believe him, but the evidence clearly showed his guilt.

"That's just one email," Yates continued. "During our investigation, you'll be asked for documentation to refute Ms. Adams's claims, but in the meantime, company policy dictates suspension for anyone credibly accused of any kind of harassment."

"Suspension?" Elation at having vindicated in his own mind the emails were faked faded. "For how long?"

"With the merger, things might take a little longer," Yates said. "But we hope to wrap this up in a week or so. We'll be discreet in our inquiries, but I must warn you, Ms. Adams indicated she might turn this matter over to the police if we don't resolve this to her satisfaction."

"You mean I could be fired?" Titus clipped the words out, nausea swirling in his stomach. Someone was orchestrating a campaign to completely destroy any credibility he had, and he could do nothing to stop it.

"Let's not get ahead of ourselves," Matthews said. "We're only suspending you pending the resolution of this matter."

"What about my current projects?" Titus said. "I have several deadlines this week, including finalizing a client's new website."

His boss shook his head. "We'll have to hand those off to someone else." He pushed a notepad toward Titus. "Make a list of what's coming up this week and where the files are stored on our company server."

Titus picked up the pad and proffered pen, then drew in a deep breath to organize his thoughts. Quickly, he jotted down the list of projects and deadlines, including file folder names, then handed it back to Matthews.

"Thanks," his boss said.

"While on suspension, per company policy, you'll receive eighty-five percent of your pay and your healthcare benefits," Yates said. "If you're found to be innocent of the charge, you'll be fully reinstated and will receive the remaining fifteen percent of your salary, plus a bonus of a hundred dollars."

Titus nodded, but didn't ask any further questions. What could he say?

Matthews's phone buzzed, and he answered. "Security is here to escort you from the building. You may stop by your desk to collect your personal things."

Titus rose without comment, knowing there was nothing he could do beyond compliance at this moment. As two burly security guards escorted him to his desk, he focused on the only bright thing to come out of his suspension—now he had a legitimate reason to call Chalissa.

"THIS IS INSPECTOR MANNING." CHALISSA WEDGED HER DESK PHONE under her ear as she leaned over to search for the pen that had rolled off her desk. She had been signing forms all morning and had nearly finished the onerous task when she knocked her favorite pen to the floor.

"It's Titus."

"What's up?" She abandoned her chair to squat for better access under her desk. Ah, there it was. Her fingers closed around the pen.

"Something's happened at work."

His words jerked her upright. "Oh!" she exclaimed as the top of her head hit the underside of her desk. At least she'd avoided banging the injured side.

"Are you okay?"

"I'm fine." She settled back into the chair, dropped the pen on the desk, and rubbed the back of her head. "What happened?"

"I'm on temporary suspension pending an investigation into a charge of sexual harassment."

"What?" Titus Davis was the last person she'd expect to sexually harass anyone. If the way he treated her was any indication, the man wasn't who she'd label a player.

"One of the newish administrative assistants said I had been sending her increasingly explicit emails and texts for the last four weeks."

"From your work account email?" Chalissa opened her email to compose a message to her boss about the situation.

"No, from my Gmail account." He paused. "They showed me one of the emails. I can understand why this young woman felt sexually harassed. It appears like I wrote some pretty explicit things."

"I'm so sorry. Tell me exactly what happened during the meeting."

She listened carefully, typing the highlights into the email while her mind sought connections between the harassment suit and what else had been happening to the Davis family.

"Is there a way to prove I didn't send those emails? Could my account have been hacked somehow?"

"I will talk with our tech department to see about finding out how this happened." Chalissa didn't mention the team would also launch their own investigation to see if the allegations were true. No sense in upsetting him more than necessary. Besides, the hurt in his voice didn't seem manufactured to her. "How are you doing?"

"Not good." His tone hardened. "Someone is trying to discredit me any way he can. First the video, then these emails. And we still don't know if someone pushed Dwayne into what happened last week. Plus the man outside Sam's window and his accident and the explosion. It has to be John Miller—who else could it be?"

"Do you have any proof it's the head of Miller Construction?" She asked the question automatically, as another thought wormed its way into her conscience.

Titus gave a short laugh. "Of course not. He probably hired someone to do the actual dirty work."

"So you think it's because of the trial?"

"What else? It starts a week from today. Pretty convenient the video came to light last week. And now this bogus accusation, not to mention the scare tactics with Sam."

"Where are you?" Chalissa sent the email to her boss, her mind busy formatting next steps.

"In my car in the parking lot at work."

"Go back to the safe house. I'll be by with lunch around one. And be careful."

"That's what you and the Marshals are there for, right?"

"We'll do our very best to keep you and Sam safe." She paused, grabbing her jacket from the back of the chair. "But someone's going to a lot of trouble to smear your name in a very personal manner—and I think he'll up his game soon and come after you in person."

# CHAPTER 22

Titus swirled around, aiming his left foot at the punching bag anchored to the floor. The Marshals must have known he'd need a way to work off steam. Dancing around the bag installed in the corner of the loft apartment's open living space, he took a swing with his right foot. He'd taken up kickboxing as a stress reliever after moving to Fairfax, Virginia—a safe sport because the old Titus had never darkened the door of a gym. To his surprise, he liked the solitary workouts. Today, he got grim satisfaction out of pummeling the bag.

After being put on indefinite suspension from his job, he had driven to the safe house, followed discreetly by a pair of Marshals. Thank goodness Sam was still in school and missed his father's early arrival at home. The Marshals checked the safe house, then retreated to their vehicle parked with a clear view of the building's only entrance, giving him the apartment to himself.

*Thwack.* He hadn't missed a day of work in three years. Lining up his body, he executed a series of kicks and punches, pushing all thoughts away except for attacking the bag. Stepping back, he circled the bag, considering his next move. Thoughts of the morning's events threatened to break his concentration. He enjoyed working for Spider Web Design and had discovered an eye for graphic design and a good rapport with customers. A far cry from his accounting work. Carving out a new life in a new career in a new city with a young child in tow had taken all of his energy for the past seven years.

He swung around to the right, bouncing lightly on the balls of his feet. *Whack!* Titus blocked out every other thought except his breathing and the movement of his body. Soon, he fell into what his kickboxing instructor had called the zone—a place where everything else faded away and it was only him and the bag, the rhythm of his legs and feet as choreographed as anything Dancing With the Stars contestants did on the dance floor.

"Titus?"

The sound of his name broke his concentration and his foot missed the punching bag, sending him sprawling onto the mat. Chalissa stood a few feet away, bringing with her the spicy aroma of Thai takeout.

"I didn't hear you come in." Sitting up on the floor, Titus grabbed a towel and mopped his forehead.

"I'm not surprised. You were kicking the stuffing out of the bag." She offered a lopsided smile. "Not that I blame you, after the morning you've had. Feel better?"

He draped the towel over his shoulders. "I think so."

"Good." Chalissa held out a hand. "I'm sorry this has happened to you."

Wiping the sweat off his palm onto the towel, he accepted her assistance to rise. Once on his feet, he didn't immediately release her hand. If they were a normal couple, he'd pull her toward him and plant a kiss on her lips.

She tugged her hand free. "I'm starving."

He followed her into the kitchen. "What's for lunch?" Grabbing a bottle of water, he twisted the top off and downed half the contents in one, long swallow.

"Thai takeout from Sisters in Fairfax. I've heard it's good." She followed him to the kitchen area where two plastic bags sat on the counter.

"It is. Sam loves their Pad Thai."

Chalissa pointed to the bags. "I got Kua Gai Noodles with chicken, egg, and calamari with sriracha chili sauce for you—Mac told me you like things spicy."

"That I do, and I've been meaning to try the Kua Gai Noodles." Without thinking, he drew in a deep breath, and with it, the light scent of lavender that clung to Chalissa. An urge to take another breath, this time closer to her, startled him enough that he nearly bumped into her. "What about for you?"

"Sisters Fried Rice with chicken and shrimp." She turned her face toward him, her eyes dancing. "But I was hoping you'd be amenable to sharing. The Kua Gai Noodles smell delicious."

"That could be arranged." He leaned a little closer, then caught a whiff of his own sweat. *Back off, buddy. No woman wants to be embraced by a dripping wet man.* Moving a few steps back, he said, "Do you mind if I take a quick shower before we eat?"

"Not at all." She glanced around the sparse kitchen. "I'll find plates and silverware for our lunch."

"I'll only be a minute." Titus quickly went into his bedroom, thankful it had an attached bathroom. Ten minutes later, he emerged, freshly showered and smelling of soap, not sweat.

"I thought we could eat at the bar." She took a seat in front of one of the plates heaped with food.

"Sure." He slid onto the stool. "I'll say grace." He bowed his head. "Dear Jesus, please bless our food, and please help us find out who's behind these troubling incidents. In your name, amen."

She picked up her fork. "Can I ask you something?"

"Sure." He took a bite. The Kua Gai Noodles tasted heavenly. For a few minutes, they both ate in silence.

"Do you really believe God cares about whether or not you bless your meal?"

"I do."

153

"Why?" She toyed with a noddle on her plate, her eyes downcast.

"Because everything we have comes from God." He proceeded cautiously, not wanting to give pat answers to her sincere questions.

"Even the bad things?" She shoved her half-full plate away.

"The bad things don't come from God, but he allows them to happen because of our own sinful hearts." He sipped his water. "Do you believe in God?"

Her eyes clouded as if the sun had become hidden behind a curtain. "I used to. My first foster family took me to church. They were one of the few people I've met—until you and Sam—who lived what they said on Sundays. But then the system gave me back to my dad but left Brandon in a group home. I tried to believe God cared, but when Brandon killed himself, I was done with God."

Although he'd suspected something along those lines, hearing her rejection of God cut deeply. He'd made a decision to only date women who loved God as much as he and Sam did. He'd seen firsthand how devastating not having a believing spouse could be with Eve, but he had not cared about faith as much when he'd met and married her. Now, though, having a fellow Christian as his mate topped the list. Too bad the confirmation came too late to tell his heart not to fall for her.

"I know it seems like God abandoned you and your brother." He picked his words as carefully as his father had chosen stones when building a wall.

"Sorry, I have to get this." She reached into her back pocket and pulled out her phone, her attention on the screen. "Our theology discussion will have to be tabled for now."

He swallowed his disappointment and stood to begin clearing the remains of their lunch.

"I have good news and bad news. Which do you want first?"

Titus put the leftovers into the fridge. "Let's start with the bad news."

"The tech guys haven't had any luck so far on tracing the origin of the emails sent from your Gmail account to Courtney Adams, but they're still working on it. Meanwhile, attorney Arnold Tucci will be stopping by tomorrow. He does some work for us, so he knows you're a protected witness."

"Do I need a lawyer?"

She looked him steadily in the eyes, her expression serious. "Yes. If it were just the video, maybe not. But this sexual harassment allegation is more serious. Even before the MeToo movement, the U.S. Marshal Service has had zero tolerance for sexual harassment. These days, we can't be too careful in handling witnesses who have been credibly accused."

"And those emails provide solid evidence I was sexually harassing Ms. Adams." Titus winced. "It makes me feel sick she thought I sent those disgusting emails."

"Did you read them?" Chalissa sipped her water.

"Only one, but it was enough for me to see why she filed the complaint." He rubbed his hand over his face. "They had a folder full of them. It must have been at least a half-inch thick."

"What about your Gmail account? Did you change your password or check the sent folder to see if there were records of sent emails?"

"No, I didn't even think about that." He palmed his forehead. "I can't believe I haven't done something so basic as change my Gmail account password."

"Don't be too hard on yourself." Chalissa touched his forearm, then quickly removed her hand. "You've had a lot to deal with over the past few days."

"You haven't asked if I sent the emails."

She leveled her gaze at him. "I wouldn't be very good at my job if I couldn't tell the innocent from the guilty. Either you've been giving an Academy-award winning performance or you have no idea who doctored the video or who sent those emails."

Titus exhaled a breath he hadn't realized he'd been holding. "Thank you. You don't know how much—" He stopped as relief clogged his throat. Clearing it, he tried again. "You don't know how much that means to me." *Get it together, Davis. Don't fall apart now.*

"We will find out who's behind all of this."

Her quiet statement soothed his tattered nerves. "I know, but will my reputation weather the storm while we do?" He hung his head, the contents of the email he'd read swirling in his brain. His cheeks burned with shame. Good grief, he'd never said such things to his wife, where such observations wouldn't be out of line in the privacy of their bedroom.

"Titus." She waited until he raised his head before continuing. "I wish I could say everyone will think you're innocent of saying such things to Ms. Adams, but there will be many who will simply believe what they hear. Your true friends will reserve judgment until they can hear your side of things."

"Maybe it's a good thing I don't have many friends. Work buddies, sure. Friends, not so much. It's hard to have friends when you have to keep a major part of who you are secret."

CHALISSA SWIPED OPEN HER EMAIL ACCOUNT BUT DIDN'T FOCUS ON THE loading messages as Titus wiped the counter. His despondency over the emails troubled her almost as much as the thought the tech guys wouldn't find evidence of someone hacking his Gmail account. At least she had started with the bad news. Now they could move on to the other updates she had about the case. When he wrung out the sponge, she pointed to the living room.

"Why don't we sit in there? There are a few more things I need to tell you."

"Sure."

In the sitting area of the open floor plan, she tucked herself into one corner of the sofa, hoping he'd sit on the opposite end. Instead, he chose the chair directly across from her, leaving the glass-topped coffee table between them like a barrier. When he didn't speak, she plunged in. "The FBI still hasn't tracked down who called Dwayne before the office incident, although they did verify someone called Dwayne's phone five times from a prepaid cell."

"Which tells us nothing."

The flat tone to his voice troubled her, but she ignored it for now. "It just makes tracking the number and caller more difficult. The FBI has many resources at its fingertips. I'm sure it's only a matter of time before they have more information." No response from Titus.

Drawing in a breath, she continued. "We do know that the explosion in your house was triggered by someone turning on all four gas burners full force and placing some sort of remote ignition device on the stove."

That got his attention. "What?" He straightened in his chair, leaning forward to rest his elbows on his knees. "How did someone get in my house without the Marshals seeing him?"

"The window in the spare bedroom had been jimmied open." She hated admitting the team had missed seeing it. "The Marshals on the street focused on watching the front of the house. If you recall, that particular window has several tall, thick bushes surrounding it, plus the massive oak tree at the corner of the house, which provided even more of a screen."

"Someone came through my house and tried to blow it up?"

"The fire marshal said the gas hadn't leaked enough to take down the entire house, but it was enough to blow out the windows and cause a fire, which the firefighters were able to put out fast." She studied his face, which had paled as he'd heard more information. "Unfortunately, there's enough smoke and water damage that it will need extensive remodeling in the kitchen, dining room, and living area."

"I hope my homeowners insurance will cover it."

"Have you called them?"

"Not yet. I will tomorrow. Now that I have all this time on my hands."

She hated to give him the next bit of news. "You and Sam won't be going back to the house until after the trial."

He groaned, dropping his head into his hands. "Any other news?"

"Yes, about the video." She waited a beat, but he didn't lift his head. "The phone Janet's estate lawyer gave the prosecution with the video wasn't Janet's phone, but a duplicate made to look like Janet's phone."

That brought his head up, but he stayed quiet.

"The niece found the real phone wedged between the headboard and the mattress when clearing out Janet's bedroom. She'd sold the bed and was moving the mattress when the phone dropped to the floor."

A spark of interest lit his eyes. "Why didn't whoever duplicated the phone destroy Janet's real phone?"

"They did. Bear with me, as this gets a wee bit complicated. Janet lost her phone a couple of months before she died. So she got a new phone, very similar to her old one. She didn't use the cloud to back up her photos or videos, so whatever was on her old phone was gone. It was the new phone that was duplicated—and her new phone that hasn't been found."

"How did they know it was duplicated?"

"When the niece found the old phone, she called the estate attorney, who immediately recommended she take the phone to the FBI, which she did. The FBI had their tech department go over it with a fine-tooth comb. They discovered the original video, which Janet had shared with John Miller shortly after recording it, according to sent emails on her phone. In that video, you didn't say anything about wanting in on the scheme."

"That proves the video we saw had been doctored, right?"

Chalissa wished she could agree, but she couldn't give him false hope. "The FBI's tech team is taking a close look at both videos to see which is the authentic one."

Resignation colored his expression. She hurried on, "I don't know all the ways they can check, but they're very good at their jobs and they will find the truth."

"Yeah, but will it be before I'm called to testify?"

She had no answer. The longer she spent with Titus, the more she saw his integrity. No way he'd have agreed to be part of such a scheme. While she couldn't alleviate his fears entirely, she scooted forward on the couch, her knees almost touching the coffee table. "Titus?"

Waiting until he made eye contact, she said, "I believe you."

Her quiet words hung in the suddenly charged air between them. Neither one of them moved. Then Titus rose and, without looking away from her face, moved to sit kitty-corner to her on the loveseat positioned at a right angle to the sofa. Covering her hands with his, he said, "Thank you."

Tears shimmered in his eyes, and he seemed to struggle to speak. With a squeeze on her hands, he managed to get out, "That means a lot to me. That you believe me."

Now it was her turn to find herself at a loss for words. "I do." The declaration, so similar to a wedding vow, brought a vision of her in a white dress walking down the aisle to a waiting Titus, Sam at his side. This would not do at all. Cheeks flaming, she pulled her hands free and stood, needing to put space between them. "I should—"

Titus stood as well, putting his hand on her upper arm. "Don't go."

She stared at his hand, the warmth of his touch sending tiny bursts of pleasure through her body. "I, um, we, um..." With him standing so close, she couldn't catch hold of a coherent thought.

"Chalissa."

The sound of her name on his lips did all sorts of funny things to her insides. *Don't look up. Don't look up.* But her heart ignored what her mind screamed at her, and she raised her gaze from his hand to his face.

"You are so beautiful." His fingers brushed a strand of hair off her cheek, avoiding the bandage covering her stitches.

Her breath hiccupped as his head dipped lower, his lips hovering millimeters from her own. *Stay professional.* Although every fiber wanted that kiss, Chalissa managed to shift back, her movement knocking a book off the coffee table.

"Dad?"

At Sam's voice, she ducked down to pick up the volume, grateful for the chance to school her features before facing Sam.

"Are you home from school early?" To her ears, Titus sounded breathless.

The thought he might be as affected by their near-kiss—and surely, he had been about to kiss her—relaxed her. Replacing the book, she snuck a glance at the father and son, who spoke in the kitchen area while Sam awkwardly unpacked his backpack with one hand.

"Nah, it's already three thirty." Sam handed Titus a folder. "My teacher said I could make up the science test on Thursday, since I missed it yesterday getting my cast."

Titus ruffled Sam's hair. "Miss Chalissa's here."

"Awesome!" He glanced around the open space before his gaze landed on her, then he waved. "Hi, Miss Chalissa!"

She smiled. "Hi yourself. How's the arm?"

He shrugged. "It doesn't ache as much as it did. Will you sign my cast?"

"Of course. Do you have a Sharpie?" She joined them in the kitchen.

"We stopped at a store to get one on the way to school today." Titus reached into Sam's backpack and handed her a thick black marker. "Here you go."

Sam thrust his arm out, the blue cast nearly covered in signatures and drawings. "I saved the best spot for you." He pointed to an open space on the top of his hand.

She uncapped the Sharpie and drew a stick bird, then scrawled her initials. "There you go."

His eyes lit up at the drawing. "Awesome!"

Handing the marker back to Titus, she said, "I should be going."

"Don't go." Sam tugged on his dad's arm. "Dad, ask her to stay for dinner."

"I'm sure Miss Chalissa has other plans for dinner." But over his son's sandy hair, Titus's eyes pleaded with as much enthusiasm as his son's.

"Do you?" Sam asked.

"Have other plans for dinner?" she clarified to buy herself time to formulate a response. Common sense told her to say her evening was booked, but she was no match for the entreaties of the Davis men.

"Please, say you'll stay. Dad was going to make his world-famous pasta." Sam's puppy dog expression melted her heart, overriding her head demanding she stop the charade before she got in too deep.

"World famous, huh?" She looked from Sam to Titus. "Who can resist that?"

"Hooray!" Sam pumped his fist. "Now you two can talk while I do my homework in my room. With the door closed."

Without another word, he grabbed his backpack and fled the room, slamming the door to his bedroom.

"What just happened?" Chalissa raised her eyebrows.

"I think my son is playing matchmaker," Titus said, laughter tinging his voice.

# CHAPTER 23

Titus wiped down the counter, taking his time with the cleanup from dinner to prolong the sight of Chalissa sitting on the couch with Sam snuggled next to her. He only heard murmurs as she read his son another chapter in the saga of Hugo Cabret. Sam had spoken very little at dinner, his eyes ping-ponging between Titus and Chalissa. Titus could almost hear the wheels turning in his head as Sam gauged their interest in each other.

Chalissa closed the book, her head tilted as she listened to Sam. He loved how comfortable she and Sam were together. His heart ached that her experience came from her brother's life and its tragic end. Perhaps being around Sam would bring her healing.

"Time for bed, Sam," Titus said. To his surprise, Sam stood immediately instead of trying to negotiate for a delay.

"Okay, Dad."

Chalissa rose as well, after putting the book on the coffee table. "Sleep tight, and don't let the bedbugs bite."

Sam wrinkled his nose. "Dad stopped saying that to me when I was three."

She laughed. "Ah, didn't realize how big you were." Cocking her head to one side, she tapped her cheek with a finger. "Does that mean you're too old for a hug?"

Sam shook his head and shyly slid his arms around Chalissa's waist. "Good night, Miss Chalissa."

The tableau ignited a longing for this to be permanent. Titus allowed himself just a few seconds to dream, then firmly squashed the image. Any future relationships he had needed to be firmly grounded in Christ—and that meant at minimum, both parties Christ-followers. While he rejoiced at Chalissa's questions about faith, he needed to guard his heart against considering marriage with the pretty inspector.

"Off you go." He turned Sam toward his bedroom, then said to Chalissa over his son's head, "You don't have to leave, do you?" Had he not even listened to himself?

"Nope, I don't turn into a pumpkin until at least nine." She winked.

His cheeks warming, Titus walked with Sam, half-listening to his chatter about school. He had to resist hurrying his son along so he could return to the living room—and Chalissa.

As he helped Sam slide his pajama top on, his son said, "I miss having a mommy."

Titus tugged the top into place over the cast. "I know."

Sam climbed under the covers. "Do you think Miss Chalissa likes me?"

Sitting on the edge of the bed, Titus said, "I think she does."

"Mrs. Jennings said she liked me, but I think she likes you more than me."

"Why do you say that?" Titus flashed back to Barbara asking him out when she'd dropped off Sam.

"Remember when you didn't know where I was and I was on the train at the park?"

"Yes." Titus didn't want to ever feel that scared again when he thought someone had abducted Sam.

"Mrs. Jennings didn't like it when I asked her to tell the train

163

driver to blow the whistle three times in a row, not twice." Sam sighed. "She kept telling me to sit still and be quiet."

"Maybe you were being too chatty." But Titus had picked up on a thread of impatience hearing Barbara talk to Vanessa.

"Miss Chalissa doesn't mind me talking. And I don't have to explain things to her. She just knows." Worried brown eyes met Titus's. "But I can't tell if she feels sorry for me or if she likes me."

"I'm sure she likes you."

"Then do you think she'd be my mommy?"

The question, spoken so softly, flattened Titus like a steam roller smoothing out a patch of road. "I—"

"She likes you and you like her," Sam hurried on before Titus could respond. "Her eyes get all soft when she looks at you, like you're her favorite ice cream flavor."

Titus chuckled. "So I'm coconut chocolate crunch ice cream, am I?"

Sam rolled his eyes but ruined the effect with a monster yawn. "You should tell her."

"Tell her what?" Titus stood as Sam's eyelids closed.

"That you like her."

Titus didn't reply as his son's breathing evened out in sleep. If only it were as easy as telling a woman you liked her. But adult life was more complicated than a second grader's, and he wished he could uncomplicate things and simply say what was in his heart.

Returning to the living room, he paused to gaze at Chalissa, who sat on the couch with her head bent over her phone. Sam was right— he did like her. He liked her very much. His idea to pretend to date her had backfired big time.

"Sam down?" Chalissa set her phone on the coffee table.

"Yeah, he was asleep before I closed the door." He joined her on the couch, keeping the middle cushion between them like a barrier. A yawn overtook him.

"Maybe I should go. You look ready to drop too."

"Nah, I'll be fine. Is there anything else you needed to tell me?"
*Before I blurt out that I like you?*

"I just got an update from the FBI on Ms. Burgess's accident." Chalissa slipped off her shoes and angled her body to face him, tucking her feet underneath her. "The prosecutor had gone to get a statement from Janet's niece about finding the phone. She left the house around seven fifteen. On her way home, a deer bounded out of the woods along the road. Apparently, Burgess swerved to avoid hitting it and rammed into a tree."

"Then it truly was an accident?"

"As far as the FBI can tell. A neighbor witnessed the crash, as did a passing motorist who had narrowly missed hitting the deer too."

He digested the information. "What about her vehicle? Any signs of tampering?"

"The FBI lab is going over her SUV, but so far, the techs haven't found anything suspicious. She'd received a text right before the crash, so the current theory is she glanced at her phone, then didn't see the deer until it was too late to do anything but swerve into the trees."

"Is it weird I feel relieved it was an accident?" He shoved his fingers through his hair.

"It's a natural reaction, considering what's been happening. In fact, I've—" Rather than finishing her sentence, she put a finger to her lips and rose, one hand extracting her weapon from its waist clip. Without shoes, her feet made no sound as she moved across the open expanse toward the front door.

Then Titus heard a soft scraping noise. It took him a few seconds to place it—the sound of someone fiddling with the lock, as if trying to fit in a key...or to pick the lock. Rising, he caught Chalissa's eye and nodded toward Sam's room.

She pointed to his phone, then cocked her head in the direction of the street outside. Understanding her request to alert the Marshals in the vehicle outside, he pulled out his phone and nodded again before slipping into Sam's room, leaving the door cracked.

Quickly, he pulled up Marshal Glenn's info and typed in a text: *Someone at front door. Chalissa checking it out. I'm in Sam's room with him.*

Titus waited, listening to Sam's even breathing and praying for Chalissa's safety and for resolution of this cat-and-mouse game. With a frown, he checked the phone screen. No responding text. He sent one to the other Marshal, then another one to Mac. Something wasn't right. Phone in hand, he eased closer to the crack in the door and strained to hear anything. Silence.

Then a gunshot shattered the quiet.

THE SHOT STARTLED CHALISSA, BUT SHE MANAGED TO STAY STILL IN her position to the right of the doorjamb. On the other side of the loft door, something fell to the floor with a jingle, followed by running feet.

The shot hadn't come from inside the building, but it had scared away whoever was trying to enter the apartment. Double-checking the security chain, floor deadbolt, and triple door locks, she quickly went to Sam's room.

Titus met her right outside his son's room. "Was that a shot?"

"Yes, outside in the street, I think." She peered past him into the dark room. "Sam okay?"

"Sleeping like a rock. I texted the Marshals outside and Mac, but received no answer." His worried eyes met hers.

"Let me check the room." She pushed past him and did a quick sweep but found nothing out of the ordinary. Without standing in front of the window, she peeked through the blinds. Sam's room offered a bird's-eye view of the building's parking lot and side street. A flash of movement from the building's back exit caught her eye. Someone walked briskly away from the building, head down and hoodie up.

A few feet away, a figure rose up from behind a parked car, gun extended. The first person hesitated an instant before bolting in the opposite direction. A third person, also with a gun, popped up from behind another vehicle parked closer to the street, shouting something. This time, the street light illuminated the back of the figure's jacket enough for Chalissa to see the words "U.S. Marshal" emblazoned in bright yellow. Another shot rang out. The running figure jerked, then dropped to the ground.

Motioning for Titus to follow her out of Sam's room, she waited until they were back in the kitchen to relate what had happened. "It looks like the guard detail have detained the suspect," she said. "But you need to stay with Sam while I check in."

She eased the door closed behind her, punching in Deputy Wong's number. "Ma'am, it's Inspector Manning. I'm with Titus Davis in the safe house."

"A little bit of excitement going on there tonight," Wong said.

"We're in the dark about that."

"Glenn spotted someone acting furtive go into the building and followed him to your floor. He called for backup, then observed the man trying to pick the lock on the safe house front door."

"I heard him," she said.

"The suspect ran when Burlington identified herself as a Marshal, so she shot him in the shoulder. The suspect's been arrested and EMTs are on their way."

"Do we need to move the Davises?" How close someone got to breaking into the safe house worried her. How had they discovered Titus and Sam's whereabouts so quickly?

"Yes, I've dispatched two teams to help with the move to another safe house. With all the law enforcement activity outside, we should be able to camouflage the Davises among everyone else. While it appears the suspect was working alone, we can't take any chances. Be ready to move in twenty minutes."

"Yes, ma'am." She disconnected, and returned to knock softly on Sam's door. When Titus answered, she said, "Get your things together. We've got to move you and Sam to another location."

Titus gave her a tired smile. "Since we haven't unpacked, it won't take long."

The fear, uncertainty, and weariness in his eyes overrode her plan to keep her distance from him. Giving in to the urge, she wrapped her arms around him and laid her head on his shoulder. "This will be over soon."

With a sigh, he embraced her, drawing her even closer to him. For a few seconds, they stood together until their heartbeats synced as one. Chalissa blinked back tears as a sense of coming home flooded her entire body. She had longed for a real home for as long as she could remember. Being held by this man made her feel safe, protected, and yes, loved. But she couldn't contemplate such a future until Titus and Sam's safety had been assured.

# CHAPTER 24

Chalissa stirred in another sugar packet. Had she added two or three to her mug? She'd better stop pouring in sweetener before she rendered it undrinkable. Carrying the steaming cup, she settled into a chair in the conference room. Deputies Wong, Burlington, and Glenn, plus a couple of other Marshals Chalissa hadn't met yet filled the rest of the seats. Wong had her phone to her ear, speaking in low tones.

"Where's Mac?" Chalissa sipped her coffee, barely managing to avoid burning her tongue. Running on less than three hours of sleep, she hoped the liquid would jumpstart her brain.

"His wife went into labor around midnight, so he's at the hospital," Glenn said.

"I can't recall if they know what she's having?" Chalissa asked.

"A baby," Glenn shot back.

Chalissa groaned at the bad joke. "I know that—boy or girl?"

"They decided to be surprised," Burlington interjected.

Wong set her phone on the table. "Let's get started. The suspect, one Jason Deming, used to live in the building before the new owners converted it into higher-end apartments nine months ago. He's a known drug offender and one of his buddies, a guy named Dean Calvert, lived at the safe house address."

"So we're to chalk it up to sheer coincidence he happened to pick the lock of a U.S. Marshal safe house with a witness inside?" Glenn asked.

"As much as it pains me to say, I think so." Wong opened the folder. "We'll keep looking into Jason's background and recent movements, but we do know he just finished a nine-month stint on a heroin possession charge. Released yesterday morning from the county jail. With nowhere else to go, he headed to Dean's apartment after scoring some smack and booze. Didn't realize Dean had moved, but in his high state, decided to pick the lock to enter when his key didn't work. The gunshot from the fracas across the street spoked him into running, and that's when he was caught."

Chalissa finished her coffee, her mind still sluggish. "We're right back to square one on who is behind the other attacks on the Davises."

"Looks that way," Wong said.

"What if we're starting with the wrong assumption?" Chalissa voiced what had been niggling at her ever since Sam's accident.

"What do you mean?" Burlington asked.

"Because of the doctored video clip purporting to show Titus's compliance with the scheme, we've assumed this has all been related to the upcoming trial. What if there's another reason?"

"What other reason could there be?" Glenn threw out.

Maybe her lack of sleep made her see connections where there weren't any, but since they were coming up empty anyway, she'd try to speak coherently. "It's been bothering me that the face Sam saw in his bedroom window and the man in the Nationals cap on the rocks don't fit the violent nature of the hostage situation or the house explosion." Chalissa blew out a breath. "Maybe I'm tilting at windmills, but I think we might have two separate perpetrators."

"Lay out your reasons," Wong said, her tone neutral.

Chalissa leaned forward to press her theory. "The doctored video put us on the path to thinking Titus was in danger. The threat sent to the courthouse solidified that. But those were distant—no one needed to know where Titus was to make those threats."

"Good insight," Wong said.

The praise encouraged Chalissa to continue. "Then Sam saw a face in the window. That's when things started to get personal. What if someone found Titus and Sam for another reason, then sold that information to John Miller? That could explain the escalation of violence against Titus."

Wong frowned. "We haven't been able to uncover a breach in security. According to Mac, Davis has been an exemplary witness, always following the rules. His concern for Sam's safety is obvious to anyone."

"I agree. I don't think Titus is the leak. But something Titus said recently about his late wife set me along this path. The Davises were having marital troubles before her death from ovarian cancer. Titus said his wife confessed to having an affair and taunted him that Titus wasn't Sam's biological father."

Glenn raised his eyebrows. "You think the man in the baseball cap thinks he's Sam's biological dad?"

"That's what I'm wondering. If so, he's probably been searching for Sam ever since the Davises disappeared. And if this man accidentally came across Titus in his new life, he might take his time to make sure it was the same kid—after all, it's been seven years, they have a different last name, and Titus isn't working as a CPA anymore. I think it's possible this man was the face Sam saw in the window and at the rocks."

"Go on," Wong said.

"What if he's now convinced Sam is his son but he's astute enough to realize something made Titus change his name. The upcoming trial made front page news, so it wouldn't be too much of a stretch that Titus double-crossed John Miller. The easiest way to get Titus out of Sam's life is to let Miller know where Titus is living." Chalissa drew in a breath. "I looked over the report from the house explosion—it wasn't wide enough to hurt Sam."

Wong twirled a pen, her signature "thinking" pose. She put the pen down with a snap. "You think the explosion had one aim—to scare Titus but not to harm him or his son."

"Yes. Everything so far has been designed for maximum fright but not to hurt," Chalissa said. "But with the trial starting next week, I think this man will make his move soon to get Sam out of harm's way."

"Because someone's coming for Titus."

Chalissa met Wong's gaze. "And this time, I don't think there will be any near misses."

IN THE KITCHEN OF THE SECOND SAFE HOUSE, TITUS RUBBED HIS EYES and poured another cup of coffee. Number four? Or was it five? He'd lost count, but the strong brew did little to give him a spurt of energy. After arriving close to midnight, he'd tucked Sam back into bed, but had been unable to sleep himself until the wee hours of the morning. The adrenaline of the almost break-in, coupled with the tangle of feelings about Chalissa, had invaded his thoughts, pushing sleep to the background. At six, he'd given up and had his first cup of joe.

With his son safely at school—and a pair of Marshals sitting in a car out front—Titus had returned to the safe house. Chalissa would be arriving any minute to discuss something serious, if her tone of voice had been any indication. Gone was the playful banter of yesterday, replaced with a briskness more in line with her authority as a U.S. Marshal than her status as his pretend girlfriend.

"Marshal Manning is here."

At Marshal something-or-other's announcement, Titus jolted, nearly spilling his coffee. He really should remember the man's name, but his brain wouldn't cooperate this morning. "Thanks." Before he could compose himself, Chalissa stood beside him, her eyes troubled. Still, he couldn't stop himself from sweeping his eyes over her trim figure, admiring how the dark blue slacks and lighter blue floral blouse accentuated her curves. "Hi, Chalissa."

"Mr. Davis."

Her formality hurt, but he hid it behind a gulp of tepid coffee. Since she had a to-go cup in her hand, he refrained from offering to make her coffee.

"Shall we sit in the living room?" Without waiting for him to agree, she pivoted and made her way to the grouping of loveseat and three chairs around a scarred wooden coffee table.

Titus followed, choosing the loveseat opposite Chalissa's chair. "What's going on?"

She avoided his eyes as she set down her messenger bag and cup. Then she met his gaze. "We have reason to believe your late wife's lover is stalking you and Sam."

The statement slammed into him with the force of a forty-pound bag of cement. "What?"

Chalissa calmly repeated herself.

"Why would he do that?"

"Because he thinks he's Sam's biological dad."

"He's *my* son." Fear jackhammered in his chest. "My. Son."

"I know."

Her quiet agreement soothed away some of the fear, but then understanding exploded like a stick of dynamite blasting through rock. "The man in the baseball cap at Sam's window and on the rocks."

She nodded. "We did some digging and found a connection to Miller Construction." She reached down and pulled a folder from her messenger bag. "Brad Kingsley, age thirty-three."

Titus frowned. The name sounded vaguely familiar, but he couldn't place it. "I don't think I know him."

"He worked as a jack-of-all-trades for John Miller before, during, and after your employment there. As far as we can tell, he's still on the books with the company."

"I might have seen his name on the company payroll, but I worked mostly in the headquarters office and rarely out in the field. The company employed close to a thousand full-time employees, and during the busy construction season, another five hundred or so contract workers."

"Maybe this will jar your memory." Flipping open the folder, she held out a photograph.

Titus accepted the picture. The man had dark brown hair and brown eyes framed by thick black lashes. Facial hair covered the lower part of his face. Again, that faint stir of recognition, but nothing more concrete. "I still can't say for certain I've seen him before. What makes you think he might have been involved with Eve?"

"We ran a check on Kingsley's cell, and your wife's mobile number popped up frequently. Thank goodness, this particular phone company keeps call records for ten years."

An emptiness filled his stomach as Titus stared at the photograph of the man who could have fathered Sam. "I'd never met anyone like Eve, so full of life, so beautiful." He closed his eyes as the pain of those early memories flooded his senses. Opening them, he confessed, "Her vivaciousness blinded me to her true colors. But within our first year of marriage, the nagging started. Why couldn't we vacation in Europe twice a year? Didn't she deserve the best of everything? She pushed me to work for Miller Construction because the salary would allow her to buy more things. I tried to meet her halfway, but nothing satisfied her desire to run with the in-crowd, whatever that meant."

"I'm so sorry, Titus." She laid a hand on his arm briefly.

"I knew something was wrong, but I was working so many hours, trying to keep up with the bills." He drew strength from her presence as he continued his all-too-familiar story. "I stopped attending church, telling myself it was better to spend at least one day with my wife, but even that didn't help. We were drifting apart, then she found out she was pregnant."

The shame of Eve's reaction infused his mind. Her tears that having a baby would "ruin everything." At the time, he hadn't considered the paternity of the child would be in question—all he focused on was convincing his wife not to have an abortion. After a few days, she did a 180 about the pregnancy, all smiles and talking baby names. She insisted on a big gender reveal party, and seemed thrilled when they cut the cake to find blue icing in the middle.

He dropped back into his chair. "She had been so worried about her looks while carrying Sam, but she never looked so beautiful." He glanced at Chalissa, who had returned to the loveseat. "That pregnancy glow you hear about."

"What happened?"

Her gentle question reminded him of the stark contrast between his late wife and this honest Marshal. Eve had been as deceitful as her original namesake had in the Garden of Eden, tempting Titus to run after forbidden fruit to satisfy her desire for wealth and social position. "For a while, everything seemed normal. Eve focused all her energy on her pregnancy. Exactly on her due date, she delivered a healthy baby boy with little trouble. But Sam was a very fussy baby."

"Let me get you some water." Chalissa headed for the kitchen before Titus registered his mouth did feel dry.

"Thanks." Sipping the water, he set the glass on the coffee table and resumed his narrative. Now that he'd begun, he had to tell her all the things he'd never revealed to a single soul. "At her six-week postpartum appointment, her doctor found something suspicious and ran additional tests. It turned out Eve had ovarian cancer. Given its advanced state, she probably had it before her pregnancy—carrying Sam had obscured the disease. We tried all the available treatments, but nothing worked. By the time Sam neared his first birthday, she was in hospice."

Chalissa covered his hand with hers.

"Eve was so angry, so bitter about the cancer." Those memories of Eve's furious face, her blaming Sam for hiding her condition until it was too late. "She had little to do with Sam after her diagnosis. I knew she wasn't being rational because of the pain, but the day before she died, I begged her to see Sam one more time. She screamed that she couldn't bear it, didn't want to be reminded of the happiest moment of her life. At first, I thought she meant giving birth to Sam. But then, she said I had it all wrong. She meant *conceiving* Sam. Then it spilled out—her years-long affair and how she was going to leave me for this other man before she discovered she was pregnant."

"Oh, Titus. That's awful." She squeezed his hand.

He clung to the comfort she offered. "Turned out, she started seeing this man six months after our marriage. What kind of husband has no clue his wife is sleeping around on him for years? You know the last thing she said to me? That she prayed Sam wasn't my son, that he was this other man's son."

The poison of her words leaked out with the telling. "I was so angry I left without demanding she tell me her lover's name. When I came back the next morning, she had slipped into a coma, from which she didn't awake." He gazed into Chalissa's eyes. "The last thing she said to me was: 'I never loved you. I only loved—' I stopped her before she said the man's name because I didn't think I would be able to control myself if I knew it."

"I can't imagine hearing your spouse say those things."

Titus forced the rest of it out before he broke down from lack of sleep and the emotional rollercoaster of painful memories. "Now all that's looping through my mind is that if I'd sucked it up and let her say his name, maybe this wouldn't be happening to us now."

## CHAPTER 25

"You can't know that." Chalissa's heart ached for Titus. The cruelty of his wife must have hurt him deeply, but she couldn't let her personal feelings derail the investigation.

"Maybe not, but it makes sense, doesn't it? If Kingsley is trying to get to my son, then if I had been able to give you his name at the first incident, we might not be running for our lives."

"Did you ever try to find out who your wife had been seeing?"

"No." He scrubbed his chin. "After the funeral, I had enough on my plate for a while. To be honest, I didn't want to know. Not knowing meant I could keep pretending things were fine, that I was only a grieving widower with a young son and not a husband whose wife had betrayed him and possibly had a child with someone else."

She could believe that—it was what she had done during those first months of sharp grief after Brandon's death. She hadn't wanted to know the truth, but eventually, she'd started asking questions, pushing back on the official version of events to uncover the ugliness underneath. That knowledge, though the truth, had hurt even deeper than her brother's passing, but it had allowed her to finally heal. Maybe putting this question to rest would allow Titus to heal fully too.

"I threw myself into my work, double and even triple checking the figures because I didn't want to make a mistake in my grief. That's when I noticed the anomalies in the books. I brought it to John's attention, as you saw in the video. That was only one invoice. I had found dozens of duplicates." He picked up his empty glass. "I need more water. Want a glass?"

"Sure." She followed him to the kitchen.

He filled his glass with water from the fridge, then got one for her. "Do you ever feel like maybe things happened for a reason?"

"What, like God orchestrated all of this?" She took a sip.

Leaning against the counter, he nodded.

"To what end?" She set her glass down with a clink. He wasn't going to start spouting God's in control nonsense again, was he?

"To bring us together."

She searched his face to see if she could detect any hint of kidding. His serious expression told her the truth. He believed God had a hand in their meeting. "That's so typical."

"In what way?"

"You Christians seem to see God everywhere, and when circumstances are strange or don't make logical sense, you shrug and say, 'God's purpose.' What does that even mean?" She threw up her hands, anger at God for what had happened to Brandon coloring her words with fire. "How is that supposed to cut through the pain of this life?"

Titus didn't answer right away. "I don't think it's supposed to take away the pain completely, but I know from experience that it does lighten the load."

"That's so unhelpful." She turned her back, suddenly fighting tears.

"Chalissa, God didn't promise—"

"Us a rose garden?" She whipped around, tears dampening her face. "We are not living in a country song."

"God didn't promise us this life would be easy," he continued as if her outburst hadn't happened. "He did promise us eternal life through Jesus Christ his son."

The truth of his words worked its way deep into her heart. She deflated, the anger leaving her as quickly as it had appeared. But she wasn't ready to acknowledge it, not yet. The hurt and anger about Brandon's death had pushed her along for so long, she was afraid without it, she might not have the energy to move forward.

"I was angry at God because of what happened to Eve, how her choices and mine destroyed our marriage." Titus dabbed at her cheeks with a handkerchief. "Then I realized only God could bring the healing my aching heart needed."

She stared into his brown eyes bearing truth to his words. Could it really be that simple?

A rap at the front door brought her back to the present with a crash. She smoothed her hair back and, hand on the butt of her weapon, moved to the door. A quick check through the peephole showed Marshal Glenn on the stoop.

"Come on in, Glenn." She stepped back, glad for her colleague's presence to distract her from the uncomfortable conversation she'd been having with Titus. "Any news?"

"They got Kingsley." Glenn looked from Chalissa to Titus, but didn't comment on the tension he surely felt between them.

After relocking the door, she asked, "What happened?"

Glenn ran down the circumstances, which she listened to with half an ear, her mind still turning over Titus's words about God being able to heal the hurt Brandon's death and her father's abandonment had left on her heart. A million questions churned inside, but those would have to wait until the Davises were safe.

"He's being brought into the local police station for questioning to avoid blowing Davis's cover," Glenn concluded.

Chalissa shook her head slightly to kick her brain back into gear. Suspect. Questioning. "Who's questioning him?"

"The FBI is sending over a couple of agents, but they're willing to play nice with us. Wong wants you to sit in on the interrogation, since you're the Davis point of contact."

"Which station is Kingsley at?"

"I'll text it to you." Glenn tapped a few keys. "A second team is coming over to stay inside the safe house with Davis while you're out."

Titus folded his arms across his chest as she grabbed her bag, shoving folders back inside. She could feel his eyes on her, as if he knew she was running away from him and their discussion. But her boss told her to go.

"And a team is already keeping an eye on Sam at school?" She shouldered the bag, checking her phone to make sure she'd received the address.

"Yes. No suspicious activity there. I'll stay inside with Davis," Glenn said.

Without looking at Titus, she said, "Would you have someone run a DNA swab test on both Davises? We need to expedite the results."

"Sure, I'll make some calls." Glenn moved away, his phone out.

Titus stepped toward her. "Stay safe."

"I will." She couldn't avoid his gaze, her heart stuttering at the compassion and another emotion she didn't want to identify. "You too." Glenn's voice drifted from the living room. With one last glance at Titus, she slipped out the door.

AFTER CHALISSA LEFT, TITUS TIDIED THE NEARLY SPOTLESS KITCHEN, restless and uneasy. His conversation with Chalissa replayed in his mind. The hurt and anger at God he had immediately recognized—after all, it had been what he'd felt in his own heart after Eve's death and infidelity. Returning to the living room, he sank into the chair and tried to read a Teddy Roosevelt biography on his e-reader. But the words kept jumping around on the page as his mind ping-ponged from Chalissa to Eve to Sam. A knock at the door made him jump.

Glenn answered, his voice a low hum. He walked a small man carrying a bulky briefcase over to Titus. "Davis, the tech is here for your cheek swab."

Titus nodded.

The tech snapped on gloves. "I'll just swab the inside of your cheek," he said, holding up a collection stick.

Titus opened his mouth for the swab, which took barely a second. The tech sealed it up inside a tube, marked something down on the outside label, then repacked his bag and removed his gloves. "All done."

Glenn escorted the tech from the premises, relocking the door behind him. The Marshal studied Titus. "You look a little done in."

At the man's observations, the lack of sleep caught up with Titus like a tidal wave. "It's been a rather eventful few days. Maybe I'll rest in my room for a bit."

"Sure," Glenn said.

Titus took off his shoes and lay down on top of the bedspread. He'd just rest his eyes for a few minutes. A knocking at the door jolted him awake.

"Davis?" Glenn's voice had an urgent undertone.

Titus bolted upright, rubbing his eyes. "Coming." Putting on his shoes, he glanced at the bedside clock. Four forty-five p.m. He'd been asleep for nearly two hours. Sam should be home.

When he opened the door, the tension in the Marshal's stance alerted him something had happened. "What's wrong?"

"In the kitchen," Glenn said instead of answering his question.

Titus snapped his mouth shut and strode to the kitchen to find two men wearing suits gathered in the living room. Fear immediately leapt to his shoulders. "What's going on?"

At his question, one of the men in the living room approached. "Mr. Davis? I'm Special Agent Ben Rubio, this is Special Agent Clark Whitaker."

Titus shook their hands, then tucked his into his pockets. "Is Sam okay?"

"Sam is missing."

# CHAPTER 26

Titus braced himself against the counter. "Missing? From school? How long?" *Please, God, don't take Sam too.*

"We don't know much," Rubio said, "but let's sit down and I'll fill you in."

Titus allowed himself to be led back to the living room, sinking into one of the chairs. He nearly blurted out his need for Chalissa to be at his side, but managed to hold that thought back. He ached for her calming presence, her hand nestled in his, as he heard the details about Sam's disappearance.

The information was sparse. During last period, the entire second grade had taken a nature walk beside a stream located behind the school's back field and not visible from the building. A paved pathway used by the public ran alongside the stream on the opposite side. Teachers often took children out to study tadpoles and the ecosystem. But when counting the students to return, Sam's teacher noticed he wasn't there. After calling for Sam and verifying he wasn't in the vicinity, she immediately notified the school, who called the police.

"When officers arrived at the school—unfortunately, right at dismissal time—the Marshals keeping an eye on Sam asked them what was happening," Rubio said. "They then assisted in looking for Sam.

After ascertaining your son wasn't on school property or the pathway, they called in the FBI."

Titus listened to the information as if the agent was talking about someone else and not his precious son. Sam would have never gone willingly with someone, would he? But he had a kind heart and might have been tricked into helping someone.

"What about witnesses?" Glenn asked.

"We were able to keep the kids in his grade after school for questioning, but have to wait for their parents to be present. Unfortunately, it's been difficult to figure out who exactly was beside Sam right before he went missing because the teachers didn't segregate the group by classes," Whitaker said. His phone rang, and he excused himself to answer it.

"Why weren't the Marshals in the woods with him?" Titus asked, fear sharpening his words.

"They didn't know the class would be outside. Don't worry—we're tracking down how that miscommunication happened," Glenn said.

All around him, agents talked about what was being done to find Sam, but Titus couldn't engage in the discussion. A numbness invaded his body, tinting the activity surrounding him with a surreal haze. He should have listened when the Marshals had suggested moving Sam to a different school, but Titus hadn't wanted to disrupt his son's life that much. It was hard enough some days for Sam to do well in a familiar school setting.

Now he wanted to shout he was the father and he needed to be out searching for his son, not trapped in this safe house. His thoughts tumbled over like a cement mixer, stirring and stirring but never going anywhere.

"Mr. Davis?" Whitaker waited until Titus looked at him. "We have more news about Sam. Using Sam's backpack, a K9 search dog found the track your son took. The dog picked it up on the path near the stream, and followed it about half a mile away before losing it at a fork in the trail. The right path wound back behind the neighborhood next to the school while the other led to a strip mall shopping center."

"What does that mean, the dog lost his scent?" Titus squeezed his hands into fists to stifle the urge to punch something, anything, to release the building fear and anger. *Please, God, keep Sam safe.*

"It's likely someone picked up Sam at that point and carried him to a vehicle." Whitaker's face wore a grim expression that chilled Titus. "We're canvassing businesses with security cameras on the rear of the strip mall where the path ends and knocking on doors in the neighborhood. We'll know more soon."

"That's it?" Titus could hear the anger tingeing his voice. "I want to go to the scene. I need to do something other than sit here."

"I know it's difficult, but we have a lot of very good people searching for Sam. We'll find him," Whitaker said.

Titus turned away from the agent before he lashed out and said something he would regret later. He needed to search for Sam. He needed Chalissa.

As if conjured by his thought, the front door opened and Chalissa rushed in, her eyes scanning the room and stopping when her gaze connected with his. "Titus!" She crossed the open area. "I just heard about Sam. How are you?"

The concern in her eyes warmed the chill taking hold of his heart. "I can't believe he's missing." His voice broke on the last word. The tears he'd been holding back spilled over, but he didn't try to stifle them. Eve had chided him when he'd shed tears after the death of his grandmother, his last remaining relative, early in their marriage, saying the trope that "real men didn't cry," but he had no fear of the same response from Chalissa.

He wanted to enfold her in his arms, but with all the agents and Marshals milling about, knew that was a line he shouldn't cross, no matter how much he longed to.

"I know." Anguish flooded her expression. She touched his arm briefly, her compassion and something else he couldn't quite distinguish visible in her eyes.

The gesture broke his composure and tears slipped down his cheeks, as he took comfort in being in the presence of the woman he loved. Yes, loved. He'd fallen in love with Chalissa Manning, and it had taken his son's disappearance for him to realize it. For now, he let the knowledge wash over him like a gentle rain. Later, when Sam was safe, he'd examine his feelings more closely, but for now, it was enough to acknowledge to himself the truth.

He blinked to clear his eyes. "I don't usually cry like a baby."

Her eyes were suspiciously wet too. "Tears are great for releasing tension. Feel better?"

"I do." He wiped away the remaining tears from his cheeks with the back of his hand. "It sounds like someone abducted Sam."

"I think that's the most likely scenario." She dropped onto the couch, patting the cushion beside her.

He collapsed next to her. "Could Kingsley have been behind the abduction?"

"I don't think so." She lowered her voice. "We were right about Kingsley being involved with Eve. I'm so sorry."

Titus tried for a shrug but couldn't pull it off. "I thought I had forgiven her, but with all this, I realize I really hadn't. After you left, I had a long talk with God about Eve and everything that's been going on."

"And?" Hope sprang into her eyes.

"I had been so angry at what Eve had done, how she had been unfaithful and cruel, that I had conveniently forgotten my own sin. How I only went through the motions of being a husband after Sam was born. She cheated on me, but I wasn't fully present in our marriage for a long time either." He took her hand. "I asked God's forgiveness for my part and I finally forgave Eve for her betrayal."

"I'm glad." She tightened her fingers around his, then let go. "On my way here, I got the DNA test results."

Titus's mouth went dry. "And?"

Her eyes steady on his, she said, "Sam is your son."

Relief coursed through his body. "Thank God."

"Kingsley admitted to an affair with Eve, who told him Sam was his son, not yours. He said he tried to find you after you left the area, but couldn't. Three years ago, he moved to Northern Virginia to work for another construction company."

"Wait, he's not still working for John Miller?"

"Not according to his statement. Kingsley said Miller had become too entrenched with the Yanovich family, which demanded more and more from Miller. Apparently, Kingsley has a conscience after all because there were things he saw that made him pull a disappearing act of his own."

Titus tried to digest the information, but worry about Sam invaded his thoughts constantly.

"He's actually going into witness protection to testify against Miller Construction," Chalissa said.

The words jolted him back to the conversation at hand. "That's good news, right?"

"The federal prosecutors seem pleased. I think he knows even more dirt than your testimony would provide."

"Does that mean Miller didn't send Kingsley to find me?"

"Not according to Kingsley." Chalissa shook her head. "It's one of those weird coincidences. Kingsley just happened to see you picking up Sam from a soccer game a couple of months ago. It took him a while to track you down, but once he knew where to look for you—and finding out where Sam's team would be playing was easy to discover—he simply followed you home."

"Was he responsible for spooking Sam?"

"He admitted to being the face in the window and at the rocks. He also said he gave the boys on the lake dynamite to fish with and broke the taillights of your SUV and the other cars in the restaurant parking lot, plus set off the explosion in your house. Kingsley says he was hoping to scare you into giving up Sam to him after he confronted you with evidence of his relationship with Eve."

"He thought I'd just hand Sam over to him?" He shook his head.

"That's his story. It appears he allowed his grief over losing Eve to fester into an obsession that fueled these misguided attempts to convince you Sam wasn't safe with you," Chalissa said. "He also told us he needed some cash to leave the area once he had Sam, and he figured out that you had changed your name for a reason. Only he pegged it at your having embezzled money from Miller Construction, not that you were testifying against the company. Long story short, he called Miller and offered your location for $200,000. Miller was delighted to make such an exchange."

Titus tried to process everything but it was hard to think straight with Sam missing. A couple of key pieces were missing from Kingsley's narrative. "What about Dwayne and the sexual harassment stuff? Was that Kingsley too?"

"No, he swears he had nothing to do with that. He told Miller where you worked. Now that our IT department has a more definitive place to look, it appears on the surface that Miller was behind Dwayne's bomb attempt and the sexual harassment." She sighed. "They were hedging their bets—if Dwayne killed you along with your coworkers with his bomb, problem solved. But if not, they had already set in motion a sexual harassment charge to further discredit you and your testimony."

Titus's mind swirled as he asked the one question that mattered most to him. "Is Kingsley behind Sam's abduction?"

"We don't think so, because Kingsley's been in police custody for hours," said Rubio as he joined Chalissa and Titus. "We do have news about Sam."

Something in the FBI agent's eyes told Titus to brace himself for bad news. "What is it?"

"A ransom note has been delivered to your house."

# CHAPTER 27

S am, kidnapped? Having his fears confirmed knocked Titus back against the couch cushions. Chalissa and Rubio stared at him, concern etched on their faces. He licked dry lips. "Did the agents watching the house get the delivery person?"

"Yeah, it was the mail carrier," Rubio said.

"The ransom note was mailed?" Chalissa said. "That's really old school."

"It was an overnight letter from a fake return address. The ransom note itself is printed from a computer," the FBI agent said.

Titus let Chalissa ask the pertinent questions. He just wanted to know what he had to do to get Sam back. The FBI agent talked a bit more about the method of delivery. *Lord, keep Sam safe. Bring him back to me. Don't let him be too afraid.*

Rubio pulled out his tablet. "Here's the text of the ransom note." He handed the tablet to Chalissa, who huddled close to Titus to share the screen.

The two short sentences made his heart stutter: *If you testify, you'll never see your son again. Proof of life will be emailed at seven p.m. tonight.*

Chalissa gave the tablet to the agent. "This appears to tie Sam's abduction to the trial, which starts on Monday."

"It seems to be a clear connection," Rubio agreed.

"Which must mean Titus's testimony is very damaging to their case," she said. "That's not quite the impression I got today from the federal prosecutors."

Titus shook his head to clear his mind, shoving his fear for Sam's safety down. If talking about the trial strategy would help bring Sam home, then he'd spill his guts. "Burgess told me when I entered the program that my testimony would be one of the key cornerstones in their case. However, I hadn't discussed my role in years as they built their case. I had a meeting scheduled for tomorrow afternoon to go over my testimony."

Chalissa drew out her phone. "Let me see if we can get an update. Kingsley is singing a lovely song, one that might make your testimony not as crucial." She selected a contact and tapped the screen. "Hello, Mr. Powell? It's Inspector Manning. I'm with Titus Davis and a slew of Marshals and FBI agents. Davis's son was kidnapped a few hours ago." She listened for a moment, then said, "I'm going to put you on speaker."

"Mr. Davis, I'm so sorry to hear about your son," Powell said.

"Thank you," Titus said.

Chalissa asked the FBI agent to read the ransom note. "Has your office been informed about Brad Kingsley and his willingness to testify against Miller Construction?"

"Yes, we have a local prosecutor there now, finding out a rough outline of what Kingsley knows," Powell said. "We were working on a motion for a postponement given the new evidence provided by Kingsley, but the defense team beat us to it with their own motion for an extension.

"When was that motion filed?" Chalissa said.

"Four-thirty this afternoon," Powell replied.

"Right around the time we realized Sam had been kidnapped," Chalissa noted.

"Did the judge grant the motion?" Rubio said.

"Since we didn't object, yes," Powell said. "I think the defense was surprised we didn't push for the original trial date, but a two-week extension will give us enough time to investigate Kingsley's claims and prep him as a witness."

"Does Kingsley's testimony change anything about Titus, er Mr. Davis's, testimony?" Pink brushed across Chalissa's cheeks at her use of his first name. The blush gave Titus hope she felt something as real between them as he did. He tucked that thought away until after Sam's safe return.

"Mr. Davis is still an important witness, but our case is much stronger with Kingsley's additional testimony," Powell said.

"When will the defense know about Kingsley?" asked Rubio.

"We are supposed to add a new witness to the list as soon as possible, but with the weekend approaching, we can stretch it into next week," Powell said.

"Would releasing his name sooner hurt your preparation or the trial?" Chalissa asked. Titus guessed she was thinking the same thing he was—if whoever had Sam knew there was another witness who would collaborate Titus's testimony and provide even more damaging evidence, they lost their leverage over Titus and would hopefully return Sam unharmed.

"It wouldn't, since we have Kingsley in custody and will be offering him witness protection," Powell said.

"Then would your office object to releasing a press release about Kingsley and giving a hint about his testimony?" Rubio said. "It could help facilitate the safe return of Sam."

"I don't see why not. We can do that within the hour," the prosecutor responded.

"Thanks. Text me at this number when it's out." Rubio rattled off his cell number, then said goodbye before ending the call. "Let's see where we're at on finding Sam."

He and the other agents huddled together around the kitchen

island, sipping coffee and talking about developments in hushed voices.

Chalissa stayed with Titus. "How are you holding up?"

"How do I look like I'm holding up?" Titus tried for a light tone but it came out more forlorn.

"Like a dad who's worried about his missing son." She put her hand on his shoulder. "We'll find Sam."

As Titus sat beside her drawing strength from her presence, a prayer circled round in his brain—*Keep Sam safe, keep Sam safe.*

"TITUS?" CHALISSA TOUCHED THE SLEEPING MAN ON HIS SHOULDER, trying to wake him without startling him. The promised proof of life email had never materialized last night. The agony of not knowing his son's whereabouts darkened the hollows under Titus's eyes. He'd eaten very little at dinner, retreating to his bedroom around nine.

She'd longed to comfort him, but had no words to say. At eleven, her boss had insisted she return home for some shut-eye before returning to the safe house early this morning.

Setting down the cup of coffee on the bedside table, she shook his shoulder more roughly.

He opened his eyes, sleep clinging to their lashes before memory widened them. "Is there news about Sam?"

The hopefulness in his voice cut her to the quick. "Nothing new."

He sat up, swinging his legs over the side of the bed. "Where is he? Why won't they let him go? Surely they've heard about Kingsley and his testimony by now."

"I'm sorry." She handed him the coffee. "When you're ready, the agents will update you on their progress."

"There's not been much progress if they still don't know where my son is," he said, cradling the coffee.

"I know." She briefly touched the top of his head, then moved to the door. If she stayed, she would be tempted to offer more comfort than a U.S. Marshal protecting a witness should. Closing the door softly, she rejoined her colleagues and FBI agents in the kitchen, pouring herself a cup of coffee. But her mind wasn't on the conversation swirling around her. Instead, she took her coffee and moved to stare out the large picture window overlooking the backyard. Gazing at the squirrels and birds busily going about their springtime activities, her thoughts returned to how quickly she'd fallen in love with Titus and Sam. What had started out as a pretend relationship had moved into the realm of reality. Lately, she'd thought Titus might be feeling the same way, but now wasn't the time to explore their newfound emotions. Not with Sam missing.

*God, please keep Sam safe and return him to his father soon.* The prayer popped into her mind without her having to think about it. That was another thing meeting Titus and Sam had done—renewed her faith in God. Brandon's death had been so senseless that she had railed against God for allowing him to die. Until this assignment, she hadn't thought about God, much less talked to him, in years. But hearing how familiar Titus and Sam were with God, how Titus prayed to him like he really heard, made her reconsider her own relationship with God. Not enough to reconcile completely, but enough that she sent up prayers for Sam's safe return.

"Mr. Davis, good morning," Rubio said, his words alerting Chalissa that Titus had joined the group.

She turned from the window, her heart beating faster when she met his gaze. Did he know her feelings for him had moved into love? She dropped her eyes to study the dregs of her coffee.

"Let's sit in the living room and we'll bring you up to speed," Rubio said.

"Have you found Sam?" Titus's question cracked across the room like a gunshot. "Because if you haven't, then what is there to 'bring me up to speed' on?"

The FBI agent outwardly didn't show any reaction to Titus's belligerence. "I realize it seems we haven't made any progress. Do you want a cup of coffee before we tell you what we know?"

"No." Titus stalked to the living room, tension radiating from every gesture he made. Chalissa joined him on the loveseat. She longed to hold his hand, but refrained from such an intimate gesture.

Rubio read from his tablet. "Working with our North Carolina colleagues, we've been able to ascertain the whereabouts of John Miller. He's now in custody. The federal prosecutor's office shared their wiretap data and we discovered what we think is the CEO ordering the kidnapping. All in code of course, but I doubt he was truly ordering a forty-pound sack of potatoes to be delivered to an address that doesn't exist."

Since Chalissa had heard this during the early morning briefing for all of the agents, she tuned out to think about how to find Sam. Where could he be? And why hadn't the information about Kingsley's testimony triggered Sam's release?

Her phone's ringtone broke into her musings. "Excuse me," she said as she rose from the couch to answer the call. Unknown number. "Inspector Manning."

"Miss Chalissa?" Sam's voice nearly made her drop her phone.

Quickly, she activated the record app before answering. "Sam?"

She pitched her voice low, not wanting Titus to hear in case her own hopes had made her misunderstand the caller.

"Yes." Sam sniffled, the sound piercing her heart.

"Are you okay?" She pressed the phone to her ear in order to not miss a single syllable.

"Yeah, I'm scared. I want to go home."

"Sam, I'm going to put you on speaker phone so your dad can hear you too. Hold on a second." She hurried back to the group and put the phone on the coffee table. "Sam's on the line."

Without waiting for their reactions, she hit the speaker button. "Sam? Your dad's here."

"Dad?"

At the sound of his son's voice, Titus leaned forward. "Sam, are you okay? Where are you?"

"I'm at a coffee shop. This nice lady let me use her phone. Only I couldn't remember your number. But I had Miss Chalissa's card in my pocket." Sam's words tumbled over themselves.

"Can we talk to the lady, Sam?" Chalissa interjected before Titus could ask another question.

A loud sniff, then Sam said, "I want to go home."

"I know, buddy," Titus said, his voice cracking on the endearment.

"Hello, this is Lily Grier. Do you know this little boy?" The woman's voice reminded Chalissa of her second-grade teacher, a no-nonsense woman who'd ruled the classroom—and loved her students.

"Yes, he's my son, Sam Davis. He's been missing since yesterday afternoon," Titus said. "Where are you?"

"I see. We're at De Clieus Coffee on Main Street in Fairfax City. Do you know it?"

"Yes, ma'am," Titus replied.

"Ms. Grier, this is FBI Special Agent Rubio. I'm sending Fairfax City police to your location. Would you mind waiting with Sam until then?"

"The FBI?" Lily sounded alarmed. "I see. Yes, I'll wait with Sam. Here he is again."

"She bought me a sticky bun," Sam said, sounding like he was eating the pastry at that very moment.

"That was nice of her," Titus said. "Stay with her until I get there."

"Okay. Dad? Hurry."

"I will."

Chalissa picked up her phone after Titus had ended the call. "Come on. Let's go get Sam."

# CHAPTER 28

Titus snuggled Sam close to him on the couch in the safe house while the FBI continued their questioning. Sam had been checked out at the hospital, but it appeared the ordeal hadn't hurt him physically and his arm cast remained secure. Now, back at the safe house, Sam relayed his story for the fourth time. The basic outline of what happened became clearer as Sam talked: The boy had crossed the stream to chase a frog, which had bounded up the path a short way. Someone had grabbed him from behind, putting a cloth over his mouth that made him go to sleep. When he woke up, he was in a room with a bed, a TV, and a connecting bathroom, like a motel room. He watched TV but rarely saw anyone. A man wearing a monster mask like the rubber ones at Halloween had brought him food and told him to keep quiet, but no one had hurt him. He'd been scared and bored but could offer no other information. Then this morning, a man wearing a different monster mask had given him breakfast, blindfolded him, and taken him on a ride. Sam couldn't say how long, but the man had dropped him off in a parking lot near the coffeeshop and left. Sam had yanked off the blindfold and made his way to the coffeeshop.

"Okay, that's it," Titus said when an agent asked yet another question. "We're done. He's told you all he knows." He squeezed Sam's shoulders, relief at having him back safe and sound making him dizzy.

"He needs a break," Chalissa said. She'd disappeared after their return to the safe house, and this was the first time in hours Titus had seen her.

He'd wanted to ask her to stay but hadn't had the guts to say so. She needed to do her job, but he wanted her at his side, helping him comfort his son. That was where she belonged.

Rubio opened his mouth as if to object, but Chalissa held up her hand. The agent packed up his notes and moved to the kitchen.

"Hey, Sam. How are you holding up?" Chalissa sank into the club chair vacated by Rubio.

"Okay." Sam yawned. "Why do they keep asking the same questions over and over again?"

"Because sometimes, we remember different things when we repeat the events," she explained, her voice gentle and her eyes kind. "Like you told us the man with the monster mask smelled like cinnamon this last time you told the story. Little details like that can help us catch whoever took you."

"Oh, I see." Sam didn't sound so weary now.

Chalissa produced a deck of cards from her pocket. "I heard you play a mean game of Crazy 8s."

Sam nodded. "I beat my dad all the time."

She shuffled the cards, dealing out five cards to the three of them. Titus could have kissed her for both explaining to Sam what was happening and for taking his mind off the kidnapping with a game of cards. For the next forty-five minutes, he played hand after hand of Crazy 8s, delighting in his son's laughter and the strengthening bond between Chalissa and Sam.

Sam had won yet another hand when Chalissa's phone buzzed.

"Oh, no. Do you have to get that?" Sam's disappointment mirrored his own.

"Yep, I do, but I'll be quick. I want a rematch—you've been

trouncing both of us!" Chalissa winked at Sam as she stood to answer the call.

"Dad, you like her, don't you?" Sam kept his eyes on the cards as he awkwardly shuffled them.

"Yeah, I do." Titus paused, but before he could ask Sam what he thought of Chalissa, his son asked another question.

Sam pushed his glasses up his nose. "Do you think she'd like to be my mom?"

The longing in his son's voice touched a corresponding ache in his own. "I'm sure she would." His heart constricted. "She might, but we can't ask her that question."

"Why not?" Sam's lower lip trembled.

Titus hated breaking his son's heart, but he had to be true to what God required. "Because she doesn't love Jesus."

"Oh." Sam looked down at the cards, then up at his father. "If she does come to love Jesus, then can we ask her?"

He brushed hair off Sam's forehead. "Yes."

But before he could explain further, Chalissa returned, her eyes bright. "Good news! John Miller is taking a plea bargain. Sam, can you play solitaire for a few minutes while I update your dad?"

"Sure." Sam started slapping down cards in a circle on the coffee table.

Titus followed Chalissa into the kitchen, where the agents had been murmuring in low voices. "What does that mean?"

"I'll let Powell explain." Chalissa laid her phone on the island and dialed a number. The prosecutor answered on the first ring. "I have Titus and the FBI agents here."

"Okay, good," Powell said. "The CEO turned himself in to our office this morning, offering to turn state's evidence against an arm of the Yanovich family who have been operating up and down the Eastern Seaboard, mostly in the Carolinas and southern Virginia."

Titus couldn't believe it. His heart beat faster as potential scenarios played out in his mind, foremost being that he and Sam could stop hiding in WITSEC.

"The CEO claims he knew nothing about Sam's kidnapping until after the fact, but he does admit to orchestrating the doctored video, trying to have you killed via Dwayne and his bomb, and setting you up to be discredited with those sexual harassment emails," Powell said. "The upshot is, with the CEO's testimony and Kingsley's, yours isn't needed because you don't have any evidence against the Russian element, only that Miller was taking kickbacks from shell companies created by the Yanovich family."

Titus half-listened as Powell answered the FBI's questions related to Sam's kidnapping. The FBI had a lead on the kidnapper, someone who worked for the Yanovich family. It was over. He could return to being Titus Clarence, CPA. But he rather liked Titus Davis, website designer. Maybe he'd ask Chalissa what she thought about keeping the name Davis. Another thought chased on the heels of that one. Of course, now that he could pursue a relationship with the beautiful U.S. Marshal, he shouldn't. Sam would be devastated but Titus couldn't chance falling deeper in love with someone who didn't share his faith. The pain and misery of his marriage to Eve underscored the importance of being equally yoked together, as the Apostle Paul put it so eloquently. With any luck, she'd be pulled into another witness crisis, and he could quietly leave the program and forget all about her. His heart whispered it would not be easy, but for Sam's sake—and his own —he had to try. *Please, God, help me to do the right thing, even when every fiber of my being wants to be with Chalissa.*

CHALISSA ENDED HER CALL WITH MAC, THE HAPPINESS IN HIS VOICE AS he described his newborn daughter echoing in her heart. Returning to the living room, she spied Titus slunk down on the sofa, Sam tucked into the crook of his arm, both fast asleep. For several minutes, she simply drank in the sight of them, knowing this might be the last time she had the opportunity to memorize their features so closely.

Titus's beard needed a trim, along with his hair, but that didn't detract from his handsome face. Sam's glasses drooped down his nose, his sandy hair flopping onto his forehead. Her heart constricted at the thought of leaving them. With his testimony no longer needed for the trial, the paperwork for the Davis family to exit the witness protection program would begin as soon as tomorrow. Titus could return to his old life as Titus Clarence. Maybe he'd even renew his CPA license instead of continuing as a web designer. At least he could stop lying about his past and find someone to share his life with, someone who believed in God as much as he and Sam did.

*That someone could be you.* As much as she longed to be that person, she couldn't—Titus deserved someone who could be there for Sam more than she could with her job. She liked being a Marshal—she liked how she made a real difference in the lives of her witnesses. Titus would realize that whatever feelings he thought he had for her were the result of the pretend dating situation and the heightened emotions of the situation.

The thought brought a rush of sadness, followed by a longing to give her burdens to God. When had she stopped being mad at him for what happened to Brandon? When she'd met Titus and seen his peace even in the midst of the danger around him and his son. Stepping out onto the patio, she lifted her face to the late afternoon sun. A still, small voice whispered that she could have that peace as well, if she surrendered to God.

*God, I'm a little rusty, since we haven't spoken regularly for so long. Please forgive me for blaming you after Brandon's death.* Chalissa stayed outside for a while, allowing God's comfort to settle around her like a warm summer day, enveloping her entire being. *Thank you for welcoming me back into your fold.*

Reluctantly, she eased back inside. Titus and Sam hadn't stirred on the couch. While she and God were once again on speaking terms, that didn't mean she had a future with Titus, no matter how much she wanted to be a permanent part of his family. Turning away to leave to start the endless paperwork associated with wrapping up a witness's time in the program, she halted when someone touched her arm.

"Chalissa, are you leaving?" Titus stood behind her, his shirt rumpled from Sam's body pressing against it.

"Yes, I didn't want to wake you or Sam." She peered around Titus to see Sam still snoozing against a couch pillow.

"He's exhausted. The agents say we can go home, then I remembered our house doesn't have a kitchen anymore, so we'll grab some clothes and stay at the Residence Inn until I straighten things out with the insurance company." He raked a hand through his hair.

"That's probably a good idea." She fidgeted with her phone, tapping the device against her leg. An awkward silence built between them. She should make it easy on him. "Listen, about all the, well, you know, stuff we said to each other while pretending to date to keep Sam in the dark—" Goodness, could she make it even more convoluted? Just spit it out already. It was like ripping a bandage off—best to do it in one fell swoop than pick at the edges.

Drawing in a breath, she let her words ride on the exhalation. "We both know feelings are fickle, and whatever happened between us was the result of the circumstances." That wasn't any better than her previous attempt. "I mean, we can't, we shouldn't..." She couldn't finish the thought.

A look of sadness crossed Titus's face. "It's okay. Sam and I will be fine."

"You will?" She searched his face for a clue this was hard for him too, but his expression shuttered into a blank wall.

"God will see us through."

For once, the trite expression didn't infuriate her like it would have. She allowed a slight smile to play on her lips. "I know he will." She sighed. "There is one good thing that has come from all of this—I stopped running from God."

Something changed in his expression. "You did?"

"I finally made my peace with God. I had been carrying around my anger about what happened to Brandon for so long, I hadn't realized how heavy a burden it was. Seeing you live out your faith even in the midst of difficult circumstances made me re-examine my own relationship with God." She laid a hand on his arm, her focus on the man she'd grown to love. "For that, I am very grateful."

"You love Jesus now, Miss Chalissa?" Sam latched onto her waist, his brown eyes sleepy behind his glasses.

She ruffled his hair. "Yes, I do."

Sam let go and grabbed his dad's hand. "Then can I ask her?"

Chalissa looked from Sam to Titus, who now sported a wide grin. "Ask me what?"

Titus reached for Chalissa's hand at the same time Sam took her opposite one. The little boy gazed up at her. "Would you be my mom?"

She met Titus's eyes over Sam's head. "But this is too sudden."

"When you know, you know—isn't that what they say?" Titus swung her hand in his, while Sam completed the circle by grabbing his father's hand.

"Who can argue with that logic?" Her heart filled to bursting as she gazed at her family. The rightness of the moment made her giddy and she didn't hold back her smile.

Titus stepped closer, his eyes now shining with a love so bright, she might need sunglasses. But this brightness wouldn't burn her—it would cherish her forever. Dropping her hand, he touched her cheek, sliding his hand around to the back of her neck.

With a sigh, she swayed toward him, meeting his lips halfway. As Titus deepened the kiss, Chalissa wrapped her arms around his waist, feeling Sam's arms hugging her and his father at the same time. She'd come home at last.

The End

# AUTHOR'S NOTE

I hope you enjoyed Chalissa and Titus's story as much as I enjoyed bringing them together. One theme running through my mind while writing their story was the way God protects us—physically, emotionally, mentally, and spiritually. Our heavenly Father never accidentally drops us, even when circumstances appear to state otherwise. Through his Son's death on the cross, he has earned our trust, and we can rest assured that he knows best how to mold and shape us into who he has called us to be. But it can be difficult to see that in the midst of our personal trials, especially when those trials involve death, destruction, and discouragement in our lives and the lives of those we love.

My prayer for you, dear reader, is that you will be encouraged by this story to hold fast to your faith. If you need a little more tangible encouragement, then sign up for my newsletter at sarahhamakerfiction.com and join my Encouragement Club—it's a way I give back to my readers with a note of, well, encouragement.

## *DANGEROUS CHRISTMAS MEMORIES* (LOVE INSPIRED SUSPENSE)

A witness in jeopardy...and a killer on the loose.

Hiding in witness protection is the only option for Priscilla Anderson after witnessing a murder. Then Lucas Langsdale shows up claiming to be her husband right when a hit man finds her. With partial amnesia, she has no memory of her marriage or the killer's identity. Yet she will have to put her faith in Luc if they both want to live to see another day.

## *MISTLETOE & MURDER* (SESHVA PRESS)

Alec Stratman comes home to Twin Oaks, Virginia, after his Army retirement to contemplate his reentry into civilian life. Instead he's greeted with the murder of his beloved Great-Aunt Heloise.

For Isabella Montoya, the loss of Heloise Stratman Thatcher goes beyond the end of a job. Heloise had encouraged Isabella to follow her dreams and helped fund her studies. Now, accused of her mentor's murder, Isabella is scrambling to prove her innocence.

Since his great-aunt had written glowing letters about Isabella, Alec is unwilling to believe the police's suspicion of the former housekeeper. Instead, he works to help clear her name.

Will Isabella and Alec be able to navigate the secrets that threaten to derail their budding romance and uncover the truth about Heloise's death before the killer strikes again?

## *ILLUSION OF LOVE* (SESHVA PRESS)

A suspicious online romance reconnects an agoraphobe and an old friend.

Psychiatrist Jared Quinby's investigation for the FBI leads him to his childhood friend, Mary Divers. Agoraphobic Mary has found love with online beau David. When David reveals his intention of becoming a missionary, Mary takes a leap of faith and accepts David's marriage proposal.

When Jared's case intersects with Mary's online relationship, she refuses to believe anything's amiss with David. When tragedy strikes, Mary pushes Jared away.

Will Jared convince Mary of the truth—and of his love for her—before it's too late?

# ILLUSION OF LOVE

ENJOY A SNEAK PEEK OF *ILLUSION OF LOVE*, AVAILABLE NOW.

J ared Quinby stared at the printouts of chat transcripts scattered on his bed, willing the words to make sense. He'd been pouring over the material for far too long and now his left leg cramped, muscles bunching and twisting beneath the scarred skin.

Gritting his teeth, he hobbled to the dresser and reached for the bottle of prescription medication. Pain made his fingers clumsy and it took him four tries to wrestle it open. After dry-swallowing the Percocet, Jared closed his eyes.

His cell phone chirped, and he grabbed it from the bedside table to answer it before it went to voicemail. "Hello." A quick glance at the alarm clock on the bedside table showed the time: 2:35 a.m. No wonder he was tired.

"Oh, fantastic, you're awake." Will Fulton sounded way too chipper this early in the morning.

Lowering his voice to avoid waking his cousins, who slept in the next room, Jared said, "Couldn't sleep, so thought I would work on the case." He sat on the edge of the bed and rubbed his eyes. "What's up?"

A snore penetrated the paper-thin walls. He had to get out of his cousin's house and into his own place. Coming here seemed like a good idea two months ago, but he'd trespassed on their kindness far too long.

"I think I found something interesting. Are you online?"

"Yes." Jared leaned over and pulled the laptop toward him. Will rattled off a URL. Jared keyed in the website and watched the page load. Slowly. "It'll take a minute." Another reason to move—he needed a faster Internet connection like yesterday. The Soul Believers site unveiled itself like a bride at the altar. Will had better not be trying to set him up—he knew Jared had sworn off women after what happened the last time. "It looks like a Christian dating site."

"Yes, but this relates to the case, not your personal life." Will chuckled.

"Enlighten me." Jared tried not to take offense. His personal life was not something he wanted to discuss with Will or even himself.

"Our tech guy saw something in the chat transcripts that pointed to this site."

"Which one?"

Jared heard pages rustling. "It's labeled 'Cynthia B.,' and dated January eighth."

Jared flipped through his copies. "Okay, got it."

"Do you see the username at the top of the page?"

"Yeah. 'Wildcat.'" He shook his head. "This guy is sure full of himself, with a name like that."

"From what I've read, the ladies love his smooth talk. Maybe you should take some notes."

"Ha, ha, very funny. What's the connection?" Jared shifted on the bed to get his leg into a more comfortable position.

"The tech went behind the scenes and found Wildcat prefers a certain type of woman on Soul Believers."

"Interesting."

"He's proven to be quite an operator who has no scruples when it comes to weaseling money out of women."

Jared focused on the site, with its cheerful text promising the love of your life if you threw down ninety-nine dollars for a year's subscription. "So he's pursuing women on this site, and they're forking over their cash. That's not a crime."

"No, it's not." Jared heard the frustration creeping into Will's voice. They'd worked this fraud case for three weeks with nothing to show for it but bleary eyes and a sense something big was about to happen. The Soul Believers angle was the first break they'd had.

"Do you have a list of the women whose profiles he's visited? To find out if he's actually contacted any of them?" Jared massaged his leg in a futile attempt to make the ache go away until the Percocet took effect.

"We can figure out where on the site he's gone without contacting Soul Believers." Will sighed. "But we can't find out if he's contacted the women through the site without a search warrant."

"And we don't have enough probable cause for a warrant."

"Exactly."

Jared's email program pinged and a message from Will popped up.

"I just sent you an email with the profiles Wildcat visited."

"How'd you get those?"

"Our tech guy said he looked for patterns on outside servers, or something like that. All I know is he managed to find the information without breaking any laws."

Jared clicked open the email and scanned the twenty or so names. "These are the only profiles he's viewed frequently?"

"Yep. He's clicked on the profiles at least five or six times, spending between six to eight minutes each, which is a significant amount of time."

"I'll say." Jared skimmed the women's names.

"I'd like you to check out the women's profiles. You'll be reimbursed the membership fee. We want you to contact the women and start a dialogue."

"Whoa. I'm not so sure that's a good idea."

"Just hear me out. If we could talk to the women he's interested in, we might have a chance on figuring out what Wildcat's up to."

Jared returned to scanning the names and nearly dropped the phone when he got to the last one. *Mary Divers*. Now there was a name he hadn't seen for thirty years, one he'd had a hard time getting out of his mind. Odds were it wasn't the same Mary he'd known as a kid, but what if it was? The pain in his leg faded at the thought of solving a mystery that had plagued him for three decades.

"Okay, I'll do it." He closed the phone and sat staring at the computer screen.

Mary, Mary, quite contrary, what have you been up to all these years?

R u there?

MARY DIVERS HIT SEND. SHE PICKED UP HER COFFEE CUP AND GLANCED at the clock on her computer. Eight a.m. Since she worked evenings, she usually slept until eleven. But after awaking an hour ago, she hadn't been able to fall back asleep. Maybe David would help her pass the time.

A soft ping turned her attention back to her computer.

DAVID: U r up early.

Mary smiled. Chatting with David always made her feel better. She had gotten used to corresponding via private messaging on the Soul Believer's website rather than texting with David on her phone. The fact he hadn't asked her for her phone number made her relax more during their chats too.

MARY: Couldn't sleep. Strange dream.
DAVID: Good or bad?

MARY: Not sure.
DAVID: Wish I was there.
MARY: Why?
DAVID: To give u a hug.

Mary sat back, her face flushed. David had been more flirtatious lately, and she never knew how to respond. In person, people made her very nervous, but online, she could be a different person, one more open and sure of herself.

MARY: A hug sounds good.
DAVID: Here's a hug 4 U. OOOO. Now tell me about the dream.

Mary typed rapidly, her fingers flying over the keyboard. As she related the dream to David, she debated over whether to tell him it was more a memory than a dream. More specifically, a memory of her ninth birthday. As she wrote, she thought about how much she had wanted a bike with pink tassels on the handlebars, a bell, and a basket on the front so she could race her best friend, Jared.

As Mary waited for David's reply to her dream synopsis, she heard a whining sound, like a bee buzzing. She swiveled around in her chair to see if a bug had infiltrated her bedroom, but the windows remained firmly closed. She stood and walked over to one of the windows and pushed the curtain aside. Maybe one of her neighbors was beating the heat by tackling yard work early.

She scanned the side yard and peered over the privacy fence into her nearest neighbor's yard. She spotted no one mowing the grass. Frowning, she headed for the windows facing her backyard, but before she got there, her computer signaled David's reply had arrived. She hurried back to her chair.

DAVID: Sounds like a memory.
MARY: Busted, LOL. Dream = actual memory.

DAVID: Did you get the bike?

She took another sip of coffee to buy time to think about her answer. No one knew the reasons for her sudden move from her childhood home to this house. No one knew her parents had forgotten her birthday entirely. But that was too much sharing for today, especially since the buzzing noise had continued unabated during her chat with David. She couldn't tell him the whole truth, so she settled for a partial truth and a white lie. Her conscience twinged, but she plowed on.

MARY: Short answer: :(
DAVID: Long answer?
MARY: We moved suddenly and I got another birthday gift.
DAVID: :( :(
MARY: It's OK. Happened a long time ago now.
DAVID: What about Jared?
MARY: Never saw him again.
DAVID: Good. Was getting jealous.
MARY: Gotta go. Bee in room. C U L8tr.
DAVID: Same time tonight?
MARY: U got it. Bye.

She logged off the site and walked to the other set of windows. Peeking out of the curtains, she could barely make out a man attacking the weeds with more fervor than skill. He raised the weed trimmer over a large patch of tall grass by the patio, and grass blades flew through the air.

She sighed as she shoved her feet into a pair of Crocs. Nothing to do but march down there and tell the man to get off her property pronto. She had no idea why someone would sneak in to release her yard from its weed prison. On second thought, maybe he'd do the whole yard and she could stop worrying about the city fining her.

Mary descended the stairs and rounded the corner into the

kitchen, which had a picture window overlooking the backyard. She took a deep breath and edged up to a window near the patio. The man had moved closer to the house. Weeds around the brick patio fell victim to the whacker as he swung the machine back and forth.

Now that she had come this close to the stranger, her heart pounded. She wiped sweaty hands on her jeans. Strangers sometimes triggered her panic attacks. Her therapist had recommended several coping mechanisms when she started to feel panicky, but now she could only recall the mantra to say something that makes you feel calm and safe. For Mary, nursery rhymes brought back memories of a simpler, happier time in her life.

"'Baa, baa, black sheep, have you any wool? Yes sir, yes sir, three bags full.'" The familiar words slowed her breathing, and she could see the man wore a facemask and sunglasses, hiding his facial features. Well-worn construction boots toed the ground by the patio as he positioned his body to take out more weeds. He also sported a pair of ear mufflers. In short, the only thing she could tell about the mysterious man in her yard was that he was, indeed, a man.

## ORDER YOUR COPY OF *ILLUSION OF LOVE* ON AMAZON TODAY!